Billionaire Boss, Holiday Baby

JANICE MAYNARD

MILLS & BOON

First published in Great Britain 2017
By Mills & Boon, an imprint of HarperCollins*Publishers*
1 London Bridge Street, London, SE1 9GF

Large Print edition 2017

© 2017 Janice Maynard

ISBN: 978-0-263-07219-8

MIX
Paper from
responsible sources
FSC™ C007454

This book is produced from independently certified FSC paper to ensure responsible forest management. For more information visit www.harpercollins.co.uk/green.

Printed and bound in Great Britain
by CPI Group (UK) Ltd, Croydon, CR0 4YY

USA TODAY bestselling author **Janice Maynard** loved books and writing even as a child. But it took multiple rejections before she sold her first manuscript. Since 2002, she has written over forty-five books and novellas. Janice lives in east Tennessee with her husband, Charles. They love hiking, traveling and spending time with family.

You can connect with Janice at janicemaynard.com, Twitter.com/janicemaynard, Facebook.com/ janicemaynardreaderpage, Facebook.com/janicesmaynard and Instagram.com/janicemaynard.

For Charles,
who makes every Christmas special…

One

December 23

The calendar might say otherwise, but for Dani Meadows, *today* had been the longest day of the year. The morning started out okay. Business as usual. Her taciturn but oh-so-handsome boss had not by any stretch of the imagination been exhibiting a holiday mood.

She'd spent several hours locating hard-to-reach suppliers who were already in vacation mode. While most of the country was shutting down for a long end-of-the-year break, Nathaniel Winston, president and owner of New Century Tech, was looking for ways to increase the bottom line in the upcoming months. He worked hard. Dani, his executive assistant, matched him email for email, working lunch for working lunch.

The only place their schedules differed was in the fact that Dani left for home at five every day, while Nathaniel sometimes worked well into the evening.

He didn't expect that of her. In fact, he was an extremely fair boss who never asked anything of his employees that was out of line. If there were occasionally situations where the company needed an extra measure of devotion, Nathaniel never demanded it. Such assignments were strictly voluntary. The employees who participated were compensated well.

Dani glanced at her computer screen and sighed. She'd just received another out-of-office reply. That made a dozen in the last two hours.

Nathaniel should give up and go home himself. That, however, was as likely to happen as the snow-pocalypse forecast to hit Atlanta tonight. The capital of the Peach State got ice occasionally. Sometimes a dollop of snow. But never in December.

Yesterday had been a balmy fifty-five degrees.

Today, though, a cold front was predicted to move through. In Dani's experience, that meant a miserable rain event and temps in the upper thirties. No worries. She kept her rain boots in a tote under her desk. A sprint to the MARTA station during a downpour wouldn't hurt her.

She raised her voice to be heard above the whoosh of the heat kicking on through the vents. "Nathaniel? I'm not having any luck. Do you want me to keep a record of these calls and emails and try again the first week in January?"

A tall, dark-haired man appeared without warning in the doorway to her office. He was overdue for a haircut, but his tailored suit was pristine. Intense brown eyes and a strong jaw shadowed with the beginnings of late-day stubble contributed to an appearance that was unequivocally male.

He raked a hand through his hair, for a brief moment appearing frazzled. The show of emotion was so unlike him, she blinked. "Um, you okay, boss? Is there anything else you want me to do before I leave?"

He leaned a shoulder against the door frame and frowned. "You've worked as my assistant for almost two years, right?"

She gulped inwardly. "Yes." Customarily, she went to his office and not the other way around.

Instead of answering, he glanced around her cramped quarters and frowned. "We need to do something in here. New carpet maybe. And furniture. Make that a priority when you get back."

"Yes, sir."

When he scowled, she backtracked quickly. "Yes, Nathaniel." His name threatened to stick in her throat.

In the privacy of her own thoughts she often referred to him as Nathaniel, but it was another thing entirely to say it aloud, even though he insisted that all his employees call him by his first name.

She noted he had said when *you* get back, not *we*. Which probably meant he would be working in this building all alone during the holidays. He didn't have any family that she knew of, though anything was possible. He was a private man.

It was ridiculous to feel sorry for him. The guy was a gazillionaire. If he wanted a homey, cozy Christmas, he could buy himself one.

After a long, awkward silence, Nathaniel glanced at his watch and grimaced. "I suppose

I have to make an appearance downstairs?" The tone of his voice made it a question.

Dani nodded. "They'll be expecting you." She indicated a manila envelope on the corner of her desk. "I have the bonus checks right there."

"You could give them out."

She sensed he was only half joking. Just in case, she answered seriously, "Your employees like hearing from you, Nathaniel. Getting a perk from the boss himself is a nice way to start the holidays."

"What about you?"

This conversation was taking a turn that made her palms sweat. "Payroll put a check in there for me, too," she said.

He grimaced. "You deserve more. This place wouldn't run half as well without you."

"I appreciate the sentiment, but the usual bonus check is fine. Let me shut down my computer, and I'll be right behind you."

"I'll wait."

She took that terse statement to mean *in the reception area.* But no. Nathaniel watched her every move for the next five minutes as she took care of the brief routine she repeated at the end of every workday. She decided not to take her purse and tote to the party. It would be easier to pop back up here before she went home. Because the office contained sensitive information as well as her valuables, she slipped a key card that opened the executive suite into her pocket. If the boss got trapped at the party, she didn't want to have to wait.

At last, she stood and smoothed the skirt of her simple black dress. She'd chosen sophistication over traditional holiday colors. At five feet four inches and with plenty of curves, she tended to look like a perky tomato when she wore all red.

Nathaniel studied her in silence. There was nothing insulting or offensive about his regard. Still, she knew without a doubt that in this moment he saw her as a woman and not simply a piece of office equipment.

She picked up the envelope with the checks and handed it to him. "Shall we go?" Her heart beat far faster than it should. It was becoming more and more difficult to act normally. Feeling so aware of him rattled her. Something had to change, or she was going to end up embarrassing herself.

No one would blink an eye if she and her boss entered the large conference room downstairs together. Nathaniel Winston might as well be a monk. His reputation with the opposite sex was not only squeaky clean, it was nonexistent.

That fact shouldn't have pleased her. But she was attracted to him, and in some tiny corner of her psyche, a fantasy flourished. It wasn't as if she had any real shot at a relationship with him. Even so, his single status kept her reluctant fascination alive. It was impossible to be near him day after day without wondering what it would be like to share his bed.

Dani felt on edge as they walked toward the elevator and then headed twelve floors down in silence. Nathaniel had his hands jammed in his pockets. More than once she had wished she could read his mind. In the beginning, it was only because she wanted to know if he thought she was doing a good job. Now that she had a serious crush on him, her curiosity was far more personal.

Why didn't he date? Or maybe he did go out but in secret. Not likely. What woman would put up with his workaholic schedule?

On impulse, she blurted out a clumsy conversational gambit. "Will you be traveling for the holidays?"

He shot her a sideways glance tinged with incredulity. "No."

Poor man. She had probably shocked him. No one asked the boss about his personal life. Dani was the closest employee to him, yet she managed to be remarkably circumspect despite the many questions she had. At this point, the deliberate choice to avoid any hint of intimacy, even conversationally, was the smart thing to do.

She wanted to learn everything there was to know about Nathaniel—of course she did. Keeping a professional distance was a matter of self-preservation. By relegating the man at her side to a box labeled *boss*, she told herself she could keep from getting hurt.

The elevator dinged as the door opened. The unmistakable sounds of merrymaking drifted down the carpeted hallway. "Well," Nathaniel muttered. "Here goes."

As bizarre as it sounded, Dani thought he was nervous. Surely not. Her boss was well educated, well traveled and wildly successful at a young age. There was no reason at all for him to dread this momentary formality.

Just inside the doorway of the crowded room, Dani abandoned the man who drew attention with no more than a quick, guarded smile.

As people greeted him, she found a group of women she had known from the beginning of her employment at NCT. Several of them shared a Pilates class. A couple of others had bonded over their young children. Ever since Dani became Nathaniel's assistant, though, her coworkers treated her with a certain deference.

She didn't particularly like it, but she understood it.

As she sipped a glass of punch and nibbled on a cheese straw, she noted the men and women who had already imbibed to the peril of their careers. Dani had nothing against alcohol. Sadly, though, some employees lost all circumspection when they enjoyed the office party a little too much.

Nathaniel was socializing, though his posture betrayed his lack of ease. At least it did to Dani. He was playing the genial host, but he would rather be most anywhere else. She'd bet her last dollar on it.

Nathaniel was never too excited about the office Christmas party. He wasn't a warm, fuzzy kind of guy. On the other hand, he was no Scrooge, either. At his urging, Dani had planned this lavish, catered affair complete with an open bar. The festivities had begun at four o'clock and were still going strong two hours later.

At last, Nathaniel made his holiday toast and passed out bonuses to key players of the various divisions. His speech was wry and funny and remarkably charming. Dani had to step forward when he called her name. "Thanks," she muttered.

Their fingers brushed briefly. "Merry Christmas, Dani," he said gruffly.

"Thank you." Her throat tightened inexplicably. Boyfriends were a dime a dozen. She needed a good job more than she needed a fling with her boss. But for the last year and a half—the length of time she had been fantasizing about Nathaniel—the idea of a physical relationship, no matter how unlikely, had made it increasingly uncomfortable for her to work with him. So much so that she had actually polished up her résumé and sent out half a dozen applications already.

During her five years working at New Century Tech, she had completed an MBA at Emory. She was definitely overqualified for the job she now occupied, however working as Nathaniel's executive assistant paid extremely well. Not only that, but watching him operate in the business world, learning from him, was invaluable experience.

Time moved on. People did, too, or they stagnated. It made perfect sense to extract herself from the temptation of a possible affair with the boss, and even more sense to pursue opportunities that would advance her career.

Unfortunately, all the pep talks in the world didn't make it any easier to do what she *knew* she had to do.

A couple of weeks ago—as soon as she emailed the first batch of job applications—the guilt began. NCT was a great place to work. Nathaniel had been a phenomenal boss from day one. Maybe she was jumping too soon.

Still, something was beginning to change, ever so slightly. She didn't think she had betrayed her intense fascination. Even so, she was getting a vibe from Nathaniel recently that was more personal than business.

Or maybe it was the mistletoe and her overactive imagination. If those feelings were real, she was in trouble.

A commotion on the far side of the room derailed her wistful thoughts. The maroon and navy drapes had been drawn before the party to shut out the gray December day. The heavy cloth panels, festooned with lighted garlands, gave the room a festive feel. Just now, someone had peeked out and received a big surprise.

A rain/snow mix had already begun to fall. The usually crowded thoroughfare in front of the building was alarmingly empty. Though local snowstorm forecasts were often disregarded because of one too many near misses, apparently this one might be the real deal.

Nathaniel assessed the situation in a glance and acted with his customary confidence.

"Let's wrap this up, folks. Unless some of you want to spend the holidays sleeping at your desks, I'd suggest you head for home ASAP."

He didn't have to tell them twice. It was Friday on a holiday weekend. A number of the staff had saved vacation days so they could be off until after the New Year. Suddenly, there was a mass exodus.

As Dani watched, Nathaniel said a quiet word here and there, making sure that anyone who was impaired ended up in the charge of a designated driver.

In half an hour, the room was empty except for Dani and the boss, who stood in the doorway saying a few last goodbyes. Without thinking about it, she began to tidy the tables. Fortunately, there was not much food left. She chucked it all in a large trash container and stacked the trays. New Century Tech used a nearby catering company for all their events.

As she began folding the soiled tablecloths into a neat stack, Nathaniel startled her by speaking from behind her shoulder.

"Leave that alone," he said abruptly. "That's not your job. The janitorial staff will take care of it in the morning."

Dani turned slowly and lifted an eyebrow. "If the snow does what they're saying it will, I doubt anyone is going to go anywhere anytime soon."

"That's a lot of *anys*," he teased.

"Well, I'm right," she grumbled. "Besides, nobody wants to look at this mess when it's three or four days old."

"Do you honestly believe the storm is going to be that bad?"

The Weather Channel was headquartered in Atlanta. Dani knew the forecasters by name. At one time in high school, she had actually thought about going into meteorology as a career.

"They say it's possible. Moisture is riding up from the Gulf of Mexico and colliding with the cold air. Even when the snow tapers off, we may get ice on top."

Nathaniel grimaced. "That sounds lovely."

His sarcasm made her grin. "Look at it this way. We only get hammered a few times a decade. Apparently, we're overdue."

"Well, in that case, shouldn't you be getting out of here?"

"I'll catch the six-thirty train. I'll be fine."

"What if they shut down the system?"

For the first time, a trickle of unease slid through her veins. That thought had never occurred to her. Her car was parked at a commuter lot four stops north. What was the likelihood she'd be able to drive home even if MARTA took her where she needed to go?

This time, riding the elevator up and back down was more about expediency than anything intimate. While Nathaniel grabbed what he needed from his office, Dani shrugged into her coat, tugged on her boots and adjusted the strap on her purse so she could use it as a cross-body bag. She wanted her hands free to hang on to stair rails if necessary.

Outside, the city was eerily quiet. The snow was heavier now, blanketing buildings and muffling sound. Nathaniel cursed quietly beneath his breath when he saw the conditions. "I'll drive you to the train station," he said, his tone brooking no opposition.

"Thanks," Dani replied, not even bothering with a token protest. On a normal day, the half-mile walk was pleasant exercise. Under these conditions, she'd never make it in time, not to mention the fact that she'd be a frozen mess.

New Century Tech's main parking facility was a three-level garage attached to the back of the building. For VIPs, a private side-street lot big enough for a dozen spaces provided easy access and the assurance that no clumsy drivers would back into a high-end vehicle.

Nathaniel drove a shiny black Mercedes with all the bells and whistles. Dani had been inside it only once, when she and the boss had gone together across town to present a proposal to a clothing firm seeking to update their online presence and ordering capabilities. Today, when they rounded the corner of the building and spotted Nathaniel's car—the only one in the lot—she had a sinking feeling that Nathaniel's offer of a ride had been premature.

The Mercedes was coated with snow, and there were no marks on the ground. Either the various vice presidents had parked in the garage today, or they had left long enough ago for the storm to cover their tracks. Something about the solitary car looked odd.

Nathaniel was the first to respond. "What the hell?"

He jogged the last few feet, Dani close on his heels. They stopped abruptly in tandem. Dani blinked. "Is that a car seat?" she asked, her voice rising an octave in disbelief.

Nathaniel lifted the wooly blanket covering the

oddly shaped lump. "Good God. It's a baby." His head snapped around, his gaze scanning the immediate area. The blanket was peppered with tiny bits of snow, certainly not enough to indicate the child had been there more than a few minutes.

Dani, too, peeked under the blanket and gasped. An infant, maybe six months old, slept peacefully in a baby carrier. The child was covered from head to toe in a fleecy one-piece snowsuit, but even so, the temperatures were dangerously cold.

"Call 911," Nathaniel said, his voice as icy as their surroundings. "I'm going to look around. Whoever did this must be close. My guess is they're watching us to make sure we retrieve the kid."

Dani was afraid to unfasten the straps and take the baby out. The heavy carrier was offering at least some protection from the elements. As long as the baby slept, he or she must not be terribly uncomfortable. The snowsuit was pink. Dani took a wild shot that the child was a girl. The baby's cheeks were a healthy color. Her chest rose and fell at reassuring intervals.

Hoping she was doing the right thing, Dani removed her gloves and dialed the authorities.

* * *

Nathaniel was pissed. He'd received several texts in the last few days from a number he recognized all too well, offering veiled threats. Never in his wildest imagination had he imagined something like this happening to him. The escapade had his ex written all over it.

Ophelia wasn't actually an "ex" anything. Nathaniel had met her at an in-town conference over a year ago and spent two nights in her hotel bed. That had been the end of it. Or so he thought.

He'd used protection. No way in hell was this baby his, despite what Ophelia's rambling emails had insinuated. If she had ever come right out and accused him of fathering her child, Nathaniel would have secured a lawyer and taken the necessary steps to pinpoint the baby's paternity.

He stood in the shadow of his own building, covered his eyes to keep the snow out of them and scanned windows near and far. Damn it. Ophelia could be anywhere. What was she trying to pull?

At last, he gave up his futile search. Dani stood where he had left her, one hand resting protectively on the edge of the car seat. "I found a note," she said, holding it out to him. "I read it. I'm sorry. I guess I shouldn't have."

Nathaniel unfolded the elegant card with a sick feeling in the pit of his stomach. The contents were much as he had expected:

Dear Nathaniel:
I cannot care for our baby right now. You're my only hope. When I get my life back together, we'll talk.
Yours always,
Ophelia

He closed his eyes and took deep breaths, trying not to overreact. Women had tried to trap men with this ruse since the beginning of time. He'd done nothing wrong. He had nothing to fear.

Crushing the note in his fist, he shoved it in his pocket and opened his eyes to find Dani staring at him with a stricken expression.

"It's not mine," he insisted. "I went out with a crazy woman a time or two. She's trying to blackmail me or something. I don't know. What did the police say? How soon can they get here?"

Dani hunched her shoulders against the wind.

"They weren't very encouraging. The snow is causing pileups all over the city."

His heart pounded in his chest. "What about the foster care system? Surely they can send someone."

"Do you really want to entrust a baby to a stranger on the Friday afternoon of a long holiday weekend? Most foster families are wonderful, but you hear horror stories..." Dani trailed off, her expression indicating that she was upset. Maybe with the situation. Maybe with him.

"Fine." He sighed. "What exactly do you think we should do?"

"We?" She stared at him as if he had grown two heads. "I'm walking to the MARTA station. If I'm lucky, my route will still be open."

Atlanta's transit system was only partially underground. Unlike other major cities, Atlanta did not have enough snow-removal equipment to deal with a weather event of this size. Blizzards were so rare the expenditure would be wildly extravagant.

Nathaniel's palms started to sweat inside his gloves. "You can't go yet," he said. "I need help." The words threatened to stick in his throat. He wasn't a man accustomed to needing *anyone*. Dani wasn't just anyone, though. He was counting on her soft heart and her overdeveloped sense of responsibility to sway her.

"What exactly do you think I can do?" she asked. Her eyes held a mix of dubious suspicion and the urge to run.

Nathaniel recognized the urge. He felt it in spades. "You're a woman. Help me get the kid to my condo. Let's get her settled. After that, I'll call a car service to take you home." Without waiting for an answer, he unlocked the car and leaned in to toss his briefcase on the back seat.

Dani thumped him on the shoulder, hard enough that he jerked and hit his head on the door frame. "Ouch, damn it. What was that for?" he asked, whirling around.

"Are you crazy?" Dani asked. "You can't drive around with an unsecured infant carrier, especially with snow on the ground."

In all his emotional turmoil over realizing Ophelia had dumped a baby in his lap, Nathaniel had lost track of the weather. Now he blinked and focused on the world surrounding them. The snow was at least two inches deep already and showed no signs at all of letting up. "Good God," he said weakly. "This is a nightmare."

Had he said that last bit aloud? Maybe not. Dani wasn't giving him any more of those disapproving looks. Instead, she huddled miserably against the side of his car, using her body to keep the falling snow from reaching the baby.

"We're out of options," he said, his brain whirling like a hamster on a wheel. "I'll put the seat belt around the carrier. My condo isn't all that far. Three miles. Come on. The longer we stand here, the colder we'll be." Without waiting for his unflappable executive assistant to protest, he retrieved the infant carrier, covered it with the blanket and scooped it up.

Holy hell. How did new mothers do this? The thing felt like it weighed fifty pounds.

Strapping it into the back seat was an exercise in frustration and guilt. To be honest, he half expected Dani to turn around and trudge away in the opposite direction, heading for the train station and home. But she joined him in the car.

The wave of relief he experienced was alarming. Was he honestly that afraid to be stranded alone with a baby, or did the idea of spending time with Dani outside the office hold a certain appeal?

She was a very attractive woman always, but today—dressed up for the office party—she exuded a warm, sexy charm that made him want to forget every one of his self-imposed rules.

Though it probably wasn't wise, he took one hand off the wheel and loosened his tie. Having Dani sit so close to him tested his patience and his self-control.

New Century Tech was located in a trendy section of Atlanta known as Buckhead. Elegant glass office buildings stood amongst quirky restaurants and specialty shops selling everything from expensive watches to high-priced real estate. Nathaniel's penthouse condo offered him the privacy he demanded along with an unparalleled view of the city.

Unfortunately, today's drive was not going to be easy. Though he managed to back out of the parking space and exit onto the street, he felt the tires slip and slide beneath him. He barely managed to avoid sideswiping a fire hydrant.

With his eyes on the road and a firm grip on the steering wheel, he focused on the objective at hand. Reach his condo. Rest and regroup. What he hadn't expected was to have Dani tug at his arm several blocks before their destination. "Stop," she cried. "That one's open."

That what?

At her insistence, he eased the car off the road and parked beside a chain drugstore. She didn't pause to explain. Before he could protest, she was out of the car and headed inside. With a shrug, Nathaniel retrieved the baby and followed Dani into the store.

The kid still slept. Had it been too long? Was she unconscious? His stomach knotted. What the hell did he know about babies? Even a bad foster family might be better than what Nathaniel had to offer.

Every inch of the infant's body was covered except for her rosy cheeks. Still, she wasn't wearing high-tech fabric rated for low temperatures. The little girl might be cold. How would *he* know?

Just about the time he had worked himself into a frenzy of doubt and frustration, Dani reappeared, her triumphant smile a blow to his stomach that took his breath and squeezed his heart.

Was he simply damned glad to have her help,

or was the prospect of spending time with Dani enticing him to do something stupid? Every logical cell in his brain shouted at him to send her away. He was fine. He could cope.

Besides, though it was true he wanted Dani, he didn't "want" to want her. As long as he kept that in mind, he'd be okay. Despite his confusion and the alarm in his gut, he didn't tell her to go. That was undoubtedly his first mistake.

Somewhere, she had found a shopping cart. It was loaded with diapers, wipes, formula and bottles. He stared at the bounty of baby supplies, incredulous. He'd been so focused on getting the kid to his condo, he'd never even thought about the fact that he had nothing—zero—with which to care for a child, especially one this small.

If this were a test to see what kind of father he would make, he was already failng miserably.

Two

Fortunately, Dani didn't appear to notice his turmoil. "I did a lot of babysitting in college," she said. "I've tried to remember everything you'll need, but I don't know if I have it all. It's hard when you're not used to taking care of an infant."

"Tell me about it," he muttered. He wasn't going to admit he would have forgotten half of the items in that cart. "We're lucky somebody's still open," he said. This was a hell of a time to feel arousal tighten his body. Dani was irresistible with her pointed chin and her flyaway hair.

She gave him a cute little half frown that said she thought he was an idiot. "You should unbutton your coat," she said. "Your face is all red. We need to hurry."

"I was hoping to be home before she wakes up. If she starts crying, I don't know what we'll do."

Dani looked better than any woman should while negotiating the beginnings of a blizzard with her brain-dead boss and an unknown baby. She was average height for a woman, though her snow boots lent a couple of extra inches. Her body was curvy and intensely feminine. The clothing she wore to work was always appropriate, but even so, in recent months, Nathaniel had found himself wondering if Dani was as prim and proper as her office persona would suggest.

Her wide-set blue eyes and high cheekbones reminded him of a princess he remembered from a childhood storybook. The princess's hair was blond. Dani's was more of a streaky caramel. She'd worn it up today in a sexy knot, presumably because of the Christmas party.

While he stood there, mute, with melting snow making the wool of his overcoat steam, Dani fussed over the contents of her cart. "If the baby wakes up," she said, "I'll hold her. It will be fine."

"I hate to be the voice of reason in the midst

of your impressive knowledge of babies, but the Mercedes trunk is small. We'll never fit all that in."

Dani's tired grin was cheeky. "The guy back at the pharmacy said they'll be making deliveries until ten tonight in a four-wheel drive. Right now, you and I will take only the essentials. I stressed to him how important it is that we get our order. He swears he won't let me down."

It was no wonder. Dani's smiling charm would be hard to say no to under any circumstances. She was an appealing mix of girl-next-door and capable confidence. In that moment, Nathaniel realized he relied on her far more than he knew and for a variety of complex reasons he was loathe to analyze.

Clearing his throat, he fished out his wallet and handed the cashier his credit card.

Baby paraphernalia was remarkably expensive. Once the transaction was complete, the clerk gave Dani a large plastic bag. The two women ripped open packages and assembled an only-the-essentials collection that would hopefully suffice for the next few hours until the delivery arrived.

"I think that's it," Dani said with satisfaction. "Let's get this little angel home."

Unfortunately, their luck ran out. The baby woke up and let the world know she was hungry and pissed. Her screams threatened to peel paint off the walls.

Dani's smile faltered, but she unfastened the straps of the carrier and lifted the baby out carefully. "I'm so sorry, sweetheart. I know you want your mommy. Nathaniel and I will have to do for the moment. Do you have a wet diaper? Let's take care of that."

The clerk pointed out a unisex bathroom at the back of the store, complete with changing station. Nathaniel found himself following in Dani's wake. The tiny room was little bigger than a closet. They both pressed inside.

For the first time, Dani seemed frazzled. They were so close he could smell the faint, tantalizing scent of her perfume.

"You'll have to stand in the door and hand me things," she said. "We can't both fit in here."

"Sure," he said, feeling guilty for not offering to take charge of the diaper change. On the other hand, the baby's needs should be paramount. God knows Nathaniel was the last person on the planet qualified for the task.

Was it weird that being this close to Dani turned him on? Her warmth, her femininity. Hell, even the competent way she handled the baby made him want her.

That was the problem with blurring the lines between business and his personal life. He couldn't let himself be vulnerable. On the other hand, he would be lost without Dani's help, so he didn't really have a choice.

It was clear Dani hadn't overstated her experience with children. She extracted the baby from the snowsuit, unfastened the romper and made quick work of replacing the baby's extremely wet diaper with a clean and dry one. Fortunately, no poop…at least not yet.

Then it was everything in reverse. When they were ready to go back out into the cold, Dani hesitated.

"What's wrong?" he asked.

Dani grimaced. "I'm wondering if we should try to feed her before we start walking again."

Nathaniel brushed the back of his hand over the baby's plump cheek. Her skin was warm against his chilled fingers. "I think she can make it. She's a trouper."

"Are you basing this on your personal DNA?" Dani asked wryly.

"I told you, she's not mine," he said sharply. "The only reason we're taking her home is because of the storm and Christmas and the fact that every emergency worker in the city is covered in snow...literally."

"Okay. Calm down."

He bit his tongue to keep from making a cutting remark. Dani was helping him. He couldn't afford to alienate her, and he definitely couldn't risk wondering what it would be like to kiss her.

Outside, they faced the next hurdle. Three cars had slammed into each other right in front of the drugstore, effectively blocking the only exit from the parking lot.

Nathaniel cursed beneath his breath. "Well, that's just great."

"We can't wait," Dani said. "Besides, aren't we close to your condo?"

"I don't like leaving my car."

She grinned. "Might be safer here than out on the road."

He squared his shoulders. "I suppose so. I'd forgotten how insane drivers can be when this happens."

To be fair, the streets were a mess. Road crews hadn't been able to salt anything more than the interstates, and the swift drop in temperature had added a layer of icy danger to the situation.

In the short time he and Dani had been inside the store, the situation had grown exponentially worse. People in other parts of the country couldn't understand, but Atlanta was particularly vulnerable to weather events like this one.

After retrieving their personal items from the car and consolidating their purchases, he and Dani struck out for the final leg of their journey.

They walked in silence, negotiating sidewalks they could no longer see and trying to move as quickly as possible.

Dani had the baby tucked inside her coat for extra warmth, which had to be a damned awkward way to walk. Nathaniel lugged the carrier and the supplies. When he offered to take the child after several minutes, Dani shook her head. "I'm fine."

It was a miserable, soul-crushing slog through

ice and snow. He could barely feel his feet. Dani must have been equally miserable, but she didn't complain. Thank God they didn't have far to go.

When they finally arrived at Nathaniel's building, he had never in his life been so glad to see the doorman or the elaborately decorated lobby.

They dripped their way onto the elevator with Dani juggling an increasingly fractious baby. On the top floor, Nathaniel found his key, unlocked the door and ushered his unexpected guests inside. "Home sweet home," he said.

Dani was frozen to the bone. Her feet had long since gone numb. Though her coat and boots were nice, they were never meant to trek through deep snow for any length of time. She had struggled to keep up. Nathaniel, by all indications, was naturally athletic. He probably played multiple sports in high school and college.

They took turns holding the baby while shedding their outerwear. Dani's chic black dress was damp and rumpled. What she wouldn't give for a roaring fire and a cozy robe.

At the drugstore she had paid for a handful of personal items just in case. It seemed unlikely she was going to make it home tonight, though she still held out hope. Right now, all she wanted was her own bed, a warm nightie and something fun to binge-watch on Netflix.

Now that she had stripped off her black tights with the silver sparkles and was barelegged, she began to shiver. Nathaniel noticed immediately.

"If you're going to feed the baby, we've got to get you warmed up first. Come with me."

Clutching the little girl like a life preserver, Dani followed her boss down the hall.

The first thing she noticed was that Nathaniel's condo was three or four times the size of her own modest apartment. It was decorated in soothing shades of blue and gray with occasional pops of color. Coral cushions. An abstract painting that called to mind a Gauguin nude in the tropics. The space was silent and perfectly appointed in every way. Not a magazine out of place. No dirty socks.

Dani wanted to like Nathaniel's home, but she couldn't. It looked more like a magazine spread than a peaceful sanctuary at the end of a long day. She stopped in the doorway to his bedroom, unable to take another step.

Nathaniel, clearly unconcerned, rummaged in

his dresser and came up with a pair of cream woolen socks and some faded gray sweatpants that looked ancient. He lifted one shoulder and lowered it with a sheepish grin. "I was smaller back in high school. These will still be too big for you, but at least they'll stay up. I think."

After that, he flung open his closet and found a soft cotton shirt in a pale blue. "Here we go," he said triumphantly. "Will this do?" She caught a brief glance of neatly pressed dark suits and crisp white dress shirts before he closed the closet door again.

She nodded. "Of course."

"Use my bathroom," he said. "I'll entertain the little one."

Dani frowned. "What should we call her? The note didn't say."

"How about Munchkin? That's generic enough, isn't it?"

"What kind of mother leaves her baby in a snowstorm?"

"I think Ophelia was probably watching us from somewhere nearby. She's a little weird, but not crazy enough to bring harm to a child."

"Why would you get involved with someone

like that?" Dani wanted to snatch the words back as soon as they left her lips. It was none of her business.

Nathaniel's neck turned red. He avoided her gaze. "We weren't exactly involved. It was more of a physical thing."

"Casual sex." She said the words flatly, oddly hurt to know that Nathaniel was no better or worse than any other guy.

"I think we should change the subject," he said tersely. "Hand me the munchkin."

Dani passed off the baby and scuttled past man and child, already regretting that she didn't have the little girl for armor. Using Nathaniel's bathroom felt oddly decadent and personal. Everything was sybaritic and gorgeous. Marble. Brass. And mirrors. Those mirrors were her downfall. She looked as if she had been on an all-night bender at the North Pole.

Wincing at her reflection, she quickly took off her dress. At least her bra and panties were dry. The sweatpants were fleece-lined, and the socks were thick and warm. The shirt was miles too big, but she rolled up the sleeves. Though she was still chilled, the borrowed clothes made her feel more human.

Nathaniel smothered a grin when she reappeared in his bedroom. Wise man not to make any smart remarks. She was in no mood to be teased about her appearance, especially when it was Nathaniel's fault she was in this predicament.

"I bought a few bottles of premixed formula," she said. "It's expensive, but I didn't want Peaches to have to wait any longer than necessary?"

"Peaches? I thought we were calling her Munchkin."

"Well, we found her on Peachtree Street, so it seemed fitting."

"Fair enough. If you girls want to get settled in the den, I'll change and join you in a minute. Then it might be time for the grown-ups to eat. Are you hungry?"

"Starving," Dani said.

She made her way back down the hall and found the den. It was a more appealing room than anything she had seen so far. And hallelujah, there was a gas-log fireplace. One flip of a switch and the flames danced.

"Oh, Peaches," Dani said. "What kind of mess

have we gotten ourselves into? These are pretty fancy digs, but you should be with your mama, and I'm supposed to be going home for Christmas tomorrow."

The baby whimpered while Dani shook the bottle and removed the protective cap. The formula was theoretically room temperature, but it might still be chilled from being outside. Fortunately, the child was too hungry to care.

Dani settled deeper into a cushioned armchair and propped her feet on the ottoman. The baby suckled eagerly. Was she old enough to take any other foods? This was a heck of a mess. Maybe they should try another call to the authorities. Or even to social services directly.

Then again, it was after nine o'clock, and tomorrow was Christmas Eve.

The child was a sweet weight in her arms. Enough to wonder what it would be like if this were really her child. Dani envied her sister at times. Angie and her husband were happily married and hoping to start a family soon. Then again, her sister was thirty-five. Dani was only twenty-eight. There was still plenty of time.

She didn't know what was taking Nathaniel so

long, but did it really matter? She couldn't imagine leaving him in the lurch, even if this situation was his fault. Could the baby really be his? Contraceptives failed all the time. He acted like the kind of man who would live up to his responsibilities, but did she really know him that well? He seemed very sure he wasn't a father.

What alarmed her was how content she was to spend this time with him. Though the moment was fraught with emotional danger, she was happy to be here. Against all odds, Nathaniel had shown her his human side. Seeing him in this situation made her feel woozy inside. He was visibly shaken and yet so very determined to seize control.

His masculinity was in stark contrast to the baby's helpless vulnerability. Dani's regard for him grew, as did her need to explore what was sure to be a doomed attraction on her part.

She was almost asleep, her head resting against the back of the chair, when her boss finally appeared.

Nathaniel surveyed the sleeping child. "She seems like a pretty easy baby, doesn't she? If all she needs are food and diapers, maybe it won't be so bad to wait it out until someone shows up to claim her."

"I burped her a couple of times halfway through the bottle. She took it like a pro. I still feel bad, though. Peaches should be with her family at Christmas."

"Fortunately, she's too young to remember any of this," Nathaniel said.

"Maybe. But she has to know we're strangers."

"I called 911 again. They asked me if the baby was in any danger. I said no. They wanted to know if the mother was someone I knew. I had to say yes. The officer apologetically insisted that they're completely at the end of their resources and recommended I preserve the status quo until Tuesday."

"Tuesday?" Dani cried, startling the child. "That's four days."

"I don't know what else to do." Nathaniel ran a hand across the back of his neck as he prowled the confines of the den. "It's already the weekend now. Sunday is Christmas, which means everything will be closed Monday. If the snow has melted, we should be able to get some answers on Tuesday."

Dani stroked the little girl's back. "Poor Peaches. Grown-ups can be so stupid sometimes."

"Was that a dig at me?" Nathaniel asked. He slouched in the chair across from hers. He looked very different in jeans, a navy sweatshirt and leather moccasins. Different and so very moody and sexy.

"Not at all," she said.

"I'm innocent until proven guilty. Ophelia's note means nothing."

"Relax," Dani said. "I'm not judging you. Besides, it's Christmas. Everybody deserves a little miracle this weekend."

"It will be a miracle if I don't find Ophelia and wring her neck."

"Poor Nathaniel. Everyone at works thinks you have no social life at all. Now you may have a child."

"I'm *not* the father," he said. "Quit saying that."

"So you don't want children?"

He huffed in exasperation. "Not now. Not today. Certainly not with Ophelia. I have no idea why she thought palming a kid off on me was a good idea. I haven't a clue what to do with Peaches."

"It's not so hard," Dani said, yawning. "The

worst part is the sleep deprivation, or so I've been told," she said hastily. "I'm not ready to be a parent, either."

The room fell silent after that. Nathaniel had clearly nodded off. With his eyes closed, she was free to explore him visually to her heart's content. For years, she had seen him in suits. He was a very handsome man who wore tailor-made attire well. But here in his home habitat, tired and discouraged in comfy clothes like any other American male, he seemed more real to her.

She didn't want to care about his well-being. She didn't want to worry about him. And she most assuredly did not want to get involved with him. Life was complicated enough without adding drama and heartbreak.

Time passed. She must have dozed off herself. The drowsiness was the aftermath of being so cold for so long and then getting dry and warm. Now, though, her stomach growled when she roused. If she stretched her leg, she could barely touch Nathaniel's toe. "Wake up," she whispered. "Nathaniel, wake up."

He yawned and stretched, revealing a few

inches of tanned, taut abs. "What's wrong?" he grumbled, only half-awake.

"You promised to feed me."

His eyes shot open. A look of stupefaction flashed across his face before he got ahold of himself. "Right."

Dani rolled her neck to get the kinks out of it. "Sorry, it wasn't a dream. The kid and I are still here."

"Very funny." He rolled to his feet. "I usually order in, but somehow I don't think that's an option."

"I'd settle for peanut butter if you have any."

"That I can do."

After Nathaniel left the room, Dani stood carefully and cradled the sleeping baby against her shoulder. Her body ached from sitting in one position. More than that, she needed to walk around, anything to break the spell of intimacy that came from napping in her boss's den. Too cozy. Too weird. Too everything.

Built-in bookcases flanked the fireplace. Books of every genre were mixed in together with no apparent regard for organization. Interesting pieces of glass and pottery shone in the illumination from can lights overhead.

Nothing about the library or the art matched what she knew of Nathaniel. Curiouser and curiouser.

He returned silently, startling her badly. The baby whimpered when Dani jumped. Nathaniel didn't seem to notice. He set the food on the coffee table. "I have coffee or soft drinks. Which would you prefer?"

"Black coffee if it's decaf."

"It is."

The tension in the room increased exponentially along with the vivid awareness that Dani didn't belong here. Her presence was an accident of weather and timing. She bore no responsibility, either moral or otherwise, for Nathaniel and his surprise Christmas gift. Even if the little girl truly wasn't his, Dani was not involved in that fight.

Then why was it so painful to think about leaving this sexy man and adorable baby tomorrow?

As if he had picked up on her tumultuous thoughts, Nathaniel shot her a look as he poured coffee. "Is there someone you need to call?"

"My family will be expecting me tomorrow afternoon, though with the weather, I'm not sure we'll all be able to make it."

"Where do they live?"

"My parents are in Gainesville. My sister and her husband settled in Chattanooga for work and because they love the area. My only brother, Jared, lives in Marietta. He's probably the one who will have to come get me if I can't drive my car. Mine's a VW Beetle, so not really snowworthy."

"I see."

It wasn't much of a response. She gave up on chitchat and managed to eat one-handed. Either Nathaniel made a habit of buying gourmet peanut butter, or Dani was hungrier than she realized.

Her dinner companion prowled while he ate. The tension in his body broadcast itself across the room. Dani could understand his frustration.

When he pulled back the drapes and stared out into the night, Dani joined him at the window. All they could see in the beams from the streetlights was heavy, swirling snow. Nathaniel pulled out his phone and tapped the weather app. "Good Lord," he said. "Look at the radar."

The storm was far from finished. In fact, there was every indication it would still be snowing until the wee hours before dawn.

The scary situation had turned into an actual blizzard. It didn't matter that by Tuesday the temps were supposed to be in the midfifties again. For now, they were well and truly stranded.

Nathaniel left her and began prowling again.

The silence built until Dani couldn't bear it anymore. "Are you Jewish?" she asked, blurting it out before realizing that was not the kind of question one asked a work colleague.

He paused in his pacing to stare at her. "No. Where did that come from?"

Dani shrugged. "No Christmas tree. No decorations." It was a logical conclusion.

"I live alone," he said, his tone indicating a desire to shut the door on this particular line of conversation.

"So do I," Dani pointed out. "But I have a tree and other stuff. It makes the season fun."

"That's a lot of work for only me to see. Can we change the subject?"

"Sure." Maybe Nathaniel was a certified Scrooge. The idea made her sad. But she couldn't very well persist in the face of his disinclination to explain. His lack of December frivolity was well documented and would remain a mystery. "I *am* worried about one thing," she said.

"What's that?"

Nathaniel had finished his sandwich and now cradled his coffee cup between his big, long-fingered hands. *Oops. No thinking about hands, Danielle.*

"Well," she said slowly, hoping she wasn't blushing. "I'm afraid this little one has slept so much during the evening she'll be up all night. I've heard about babies who get their days and nights mixed up."

"I can get by on a few hours of sleep. I'll take the night shift. You deserve some rest." He stood up. "Let me show you the guest room. I guess you'll need a different shirt to sleep in?"

Three

He made it a question. Having Dani wear his clothes and wear them so damned well made it hard for him to think about babies and responsibility. He'd been attracted to her for a long time, but he knew better than to get involved with an employee. He'd learned that lesson the hard way. It wasn't one he would soon forget.

It was imperative that he get rid of Dani before he did something stupid—imperative for two reasons. One, he didn't need the temptation of having his charming, cheerful, cute-as-the-proverbial-button assistant underfoot outside of office hours. And two, he felt guilty as hell for ruining her holiday plans. Maybe they were still salvageable. She said she hadn't planned to leave until tomorrow, and Gainesville was not even two hours away.

Unfortunately, the massive and almost unprecedented winter storm was the wild card in this scenario. And then there was the baby. If he did the right thing and sent Dani home for Christmas, he'd be stuck caring for an infant. The notion was more than a little terrifying.

"Another shirt would be helpful," Dani said quietly, not meeting his gaze.

"Follow me," he said gruffly. The condo had two guest rooms. One he used as a home office. The other was furnished simply and elegantly in shades of amber, chocolate and ivory.

He'd hired a professional to do the whole condo when he bought it. Everything but the den. That was his and his alone. The huge comfy couch, big-screen TV and gas fireplace were things he had purchased on his own. Except for sleeping, he spent most of his leisure hours in the den. Ah, who was he kidding? He worked in there, as well. Creating boundaries had never been his strong suit.

In the guest room, Dani explored, the baby still in her arms. But the little girl was waking up.

Dani grinned and kissed the baby's head. "Hey there, Peaches. Mr. Nathaniel is showing me around. You want to sleep in here with me?"

It was tempting, very tempting, to let Dani rescue him. But such cowardice would be wrong on several levels. He took the baby from her and shook his head. "Take a shower if you want to. Get ready for bed. Then you can help me get everything set up in my bedroom for the night."

"Okay." Dani's eyes were big as saucers. Maybe she was worried about the innocent baby.

"I won't let anything happen to her," he said. The defensive note in his voice was unavoidable. As unpalatable as it seemed, he had to at least acknowledge the possibility, however slim, that Peaches was his. "We'll give you some privacy," he said. "When you're ready, come find us."

Dani returned to the foyer and gathered all her things. If she hung the dress and tights carefully, they might be wearable again. At the drugstore, she had bought toothpaste, a toothbrush and some facial cleanser. Fortunately—because of the Christmas party—she had made sure that morning to put mascara and other makeup in her purse for touch-ups.

After a quick shower, she rinsed out her bra and panties and hung them on the towel bar. Then she put on the sweatpants sans undies and spent a few minutes blow-drying her hair. It was thick and shoulder length, maybe her best feature. Because it was still a little damp when she was done, she left it loose. Whenever Nathaniel remembered to give her a second shirt, she would change into that for the night.

Barely half an hour had elapsed by the time she went in search of her host, forty-five minutes at the most. It wasn't hard to locate him. All she had to do was follow the sound of screaming. Little Peaches had a great set of lungs.

Dani stopped dead in the doorway of Nathaniel's bedroom, taking in the scene with open-mouthed awe.

Nathaniel's head shot up and he glared at her, his expression hot enough to melt steel. "If you dare laugh, you're fired."

She swallowed hard, schooling her face to show nothing more than calm interest. "I wouldn't dream of laughing." It was maybe the biggest lie she had ever uttered. Poor Nathaniel.

Peaches had experienced what those in the parenting world not-so-fondly call a *blowout*. A poop so big and messy it squirts out the sides of the diaper and into every crevice imaginable. It was clear Nathaniel had made a heroic effort to remove the dirty diaper and replace it with a clean one, but he was taking too long, and poor Peaches was mad.

Dani grabbed several wipes out of the container and began cleaning the spots Nathaniel had either missed or hadn't gotten to yet. The baby was stark naked. Nathaniel had poop on his hands, his sweatshirt and if she weren't mistaken, a smudge on his chin. He was wild-eyed and flushed.

Her heart squeezed in sympathy. Most parents had nine months to get used to the idea of a baby. Nathaniel had been tossed in the deep end. If Peaches weren't his at all, this whole experience was even more unfair.

"I'll pick her up," Dani said. "You start getting rid of all the nasty stuff and throw your comforter in the washer." She was afraid the bed covering was beyond redemption.

Carrying the baby into the bathroom and using the sink as a miniature bathtub was her next step. Fortunately, the little one stopped crying when she saw herself in the mirror. Dani adjusted the water temperature and grabbed a washcloth.

The bottle of liquid hand soap on the counter would have to do for now. Moments later, she wrapped the sweet-smelling infant in one of Nathaniel's big, fluffy towels and returned to the bedroom.

Nathaniel had just finished cleaning up the mess that was his mattress. He held out a fresh diaper. "You can do the honors."

"Of course. I can't believe this Ophelia person left you with nothing. We don't even have another outfit for the baby."

"I turned up the thermostat. And I put her sleeper in the wash with all the rest. It will be ready in a couple of hours."

"I guess that will have to do." Since Peaches was sucking on her fist, it seemed another bottle was in order. "I'll feed her again. Your turn in the bathroom."

When she turned to walk away, Nathaniel put his hand on her shoulder lightly. "Thank you,

Dani. I know my thanks is not enough, but I want you to know I'm grateful."

They were standing so close together she could see the dark stubble on his chin. It was the end of the day. That made sense. His brown eyes were deep pools of melted chocolate. He smelled of soap and a tiny hint of aftershave and maybe even a whiff of baby poop. Dani bit her bottom lip. Why had the baby chosen now to be docile? A diversion would be helpful.

"You're welcome," she said quietly. "I know this isn't easy. You're doing the right thing."

He shrugged. "It's not as if I had a choice."

"Even without the snowstorm, I think you would have taken the child. Because you have to know…one way or another."

"Who made you so smart?"

"Not smart. Just realistic. You're not the kind of man to walk away from a responsibility, unpleasant or otherwise."

"It's more that that," he said.

His hand was still on her shoulder, fingers splayed, though she wasn't sure he noticed. "How so?"

"What if Peaches *is* mine? Birth control is

never a hundred percent. What if this little girl is my only shot at having a child?"

"You don't think you'll get married one day?"

The hour was late. It had been a very strange day. Nathaniel was practically embracing Dani and the baby. She wanted to lean into him and rest her head. She was tired and confused and very afraid of doing something she would regret.

It took everything she had to step back and break the spell. "I shouldn't have asked you that," she said hastily. "I'm sorry, Mr. Winston." She used his last name as a shield, but it was flimsy armor at best.

You can't put a genie back in the bottle, though. Nathaniel gave her a pointed look as if he saw right through her attempt to be businesslike. "I think we have to concentrate on what's important here. If you and Peaches are really okay for the moment, I'll jump in the shower. I still smell like a diaper pail."

"No, you don't," Dani protested, laughing. "But yeah, we're fine. Take your time."

On her way to the den, the doorbell rang. No one could come up without going through the reception desk downstairs, so this must be the delivery from the drugstore. She pressed the intercom button and waited for confirmation just to be sure.

After the young teenager unloaded all the baby paraphernalia in the foyer, Dani tipped him well and sent him on his way.

"This is it, Peaches," she said, bending down to pick up the smallest package of diapers. "I hope I did the math right. This has to last us until the snow melts or your mama shows up, whichever comes first."

Of course, it didn't take a genius to guess that Ophelia was probably snowed in wherever she was hiding out. It was creepy to think a woman like that had been watching as Nathaniel and Dani spotted the infant carrier for the first time. What would she have done if the two of them had walked away? She must have been relying on the decency of human nature. Even so, Dani would never have left her own baby in such circumstances. It was too risky.

She wandered back to the den and spread an afghan on the thick carpet so the baby could have tummy time. Peaches was very mobile already and trying her best to sit up. No signs of any bottom teeth poking through. Dani guessed the little girl was about five months old, maybe six.

As the baby played with a rattle from the drugstore, Dani stretched out beside her and leaned back on her elbows. It was a strange feeling to be a guest in her boss's home. Definitely outside the parameters of their usual interactions. Up until today, she'd had no clue where he lived.

Now, suddenly, everything was different.

When Nathaniel reappeared, his hair was damp and he had ditched the clothes the baby had desecrated.

"Much better," Dani teased, telling herself her heart wasn't beating faster.

He grinned, the sudden smile taking her by surprise. Her boss was more serious than playful as a rule. "Is it still Friday?" he asked, leaning a hip against the arm of the sofa. "I feel like we've fallen through the rabbit hole."

"Still Friday. I'm guessing your life isn't usually so tumultuous?"

"You could say that." He raked both hands through this hair. "I shouldn't have dragged you into this."

"Look at it this way. You probably saved me

from being stranded on the side of the road. At least I'm safe and warm and dry."

"What a testimonial. Have you called your family yet?"

"Yes. I told them I was staying with a friend and that I would check in again tomorrow."

"Let's hope we don't lose power."

"Bite your tongue. That's not even funny."

"I wasn't joking. If we do get ice on the back end of this thing, the situation could get dicey."

"Oh, goody. Something to look forward to."

He cocked his head, his lips twitching. "How have I never noticed what a smart mouth you have?"

"I'm always deferential in our work environment." She smiled demurely, astonished to realize they were flirting. Of course, with a baby between them nothing could happen. But still...

Nathaniel stood up to pace. She was beginning to recognize his signature mood when he was agitated. He did it occasionally at work, but it was more pronounced on his home turf. "Is she getting sleepy?" he asked. "When should we put her to bed?"

"How should I know? Do you have work you

need to do? You might as well let me take care of her for the moment. It's not like I can go anywhere."

"I know, I know. And I'm sorry."

"Quit apologizing, Nathaniel. Humility doesn't become you."

"Ouch." He squatted and rubbed the baby's tummy, his gaze pensive. "She doesn't look like me, not even a little bit."

The non sequitur betrayed his inner turmoil. Dani felt her heart squeeze. "In my experience, babies this age rarely look like anybody but themselves, Nathaniel. Don't torment yourself. Until you know for sure, she's just a baby."

"I suppose." He glanced sideways at her. "Go on to bed, Dani. I'll come get you if I get in trouble."

"You promise?"

"I do."

Nathaniel sighed beneath his breath. Hopefully Dani didn't realize how completely out of his element he was. He had learned long ago—while earning his stripes in the business world—never to show fear. He could negotiate with the baddest of the badasses. What he didn't know how to do was take care of a helpless human. Little Peaches was so damned fragile.

He scooped her up. "Here's the thing, kiddo. I need you to cut me a break tonight. I'll feed you and change your diaper, but you need to sleep. That's what babies do."

The little girl stuck a thumb in her mouth and stared up at him, unblinking. What was she thinking? Did babies think about anything?

After turning out the lights, he carried Peaches to his bedroom and surveyed the furnishings. As far as he could tell, the most important thing was to keep the kid confined. He knew it was dangerous to put her in his own bed. After getting out of the shower earlier, he had spread a sheet on the soft carpet and surrounded it with several wooden chairs. He'd probably be awake all night worrying about the kid, but he'd survive.

Fortunately, the baby had worn herself out playing with Dani. All it took was a few circuits around the bedroom with Peaches on his shoulder, and gradually her little body went limp. He crouched and laid her in the makeshift bed. Poor kid. She should be with her mother right now. It was impossible not to think about the marked differences between Ophelia and Dani. One woman was self-centered and flighty...the other generous and dependable.

At one time in his life, he had assumed all women were self-centered. His mother had taught him to believe that. It wasn't true, though. God willing, this little sweetheart would grow up with kindness in her heart.

On a normal evening, he was awake until after one. Tonight, that was a luxury he couldn't afford. Stripping down to his boxers, he climbed into bed, stretched out on his back and exhaled. What a hell of a day.

It was impossible not to think about the fact that Dani was sleeping in his guest room just down the hall. He liked and respected her. In recent months, he'd stumbled upon another feeling he couldn't, or wouldn't, acknowledge.

Dani deserved to find a man who would put her first, a man who would be happy to settle down with her and create a normal family life. That man wasn't Nathaniel. He'd certainly never experienced such a thing as *normal* in his formative years. All he knew was work and more work. That focus had propelled him to the top of his career. Given his long hours and his absolute refusal to date anyone remotely connected to New Century Tech, his options for meeting women were limited.

Loneliness and sexual hunger had been to blame for his hookup with Ophelia when they met at a conference. It had taken less than forty-eight hours for him to figure out that she was a narcissist and incredibly high maintenance. He'd broken off the relationship before it started, but perhaps the damage had been done.

The prospect of co-parenting with Ophelia for the next twenty years was daunting. Depressing, even. But if Peaches were his daughter, he would suck it up and be the best damned dad he could be. Never would he make that sweet little girl endure the kind of childhood he had experienced.

Unbidden, his thoughts returned to Dani. After seeing his father's life ruined years ago, Nathaniel had forged ironclad rules for his own business relationships.

That line in the sand had never been difficult to preserve until Dani walked into his life. She had become necessary to him. He told himself it was nothing more than a good working partnership.

Now, in the darkness and privacy of his bedroom, he acknowledged the possibility that he had been lying to himself. She was here. Now. Sleeping under his roof and making him think about things that were definitely not conducive to relaxation.

Arousal tightened his body and fractured his breathing. *Damn it.* He rolled onto his side and told himself he wasn't a slave to his urges.

Yawning, he tried converting foreign currencies in his head. It was better than counting sheep. Eventually, exhaustion claimed him…

The waning hours of the night turned into a long, wretched dream. The baby woke him every forty-five to ninety minutes. He knew she was disoriented and unsettled. Thankfully, each time he picked her up and cuddled her, he was able to coax her back to sleep.

At 5:00 a.m., though, the volume of her cries told him she was hungry again. Carrying her into the kitchen, he found one of the premixed formula bottles and uncapped it. He would have to learn how to mix the powder, but not while it was still dark outside.

Earlier, he had thrown on a robe with his boxers. Now he and Peaches settled on the sofa in the den. Pulling an afghan over both of them, he leaned back and watched as the baby gobbled down her meal. He remembered Dani mentioning the need for burping. When the bottle was half-empty, he hefted the baby onto his shoulder and patted her back. Peaches didn't like being interrupted, but her loud belch told him he'd done the right thing.

While the infant finished her formula, he reached for the remote and turned the TV on with the volume muted. He had a million channels to choose from, but nothing interested him. He wanted a distraction…some assurance that the world still spun in its normal orbit. Skipping over infomercials and weird sports channels, he landed on an old movie, a Christmas film.

He had never seen it all the way through, but he knew the general premise. A man unhappy with his life wished he had never been born and then had a chance to see what the world would have been like without him.

The scenario hit uncomfortably near home for Nathaniel. He had no close friends by design. As head of the company, he knew better than to build relationships that might backfire on him. Because he worked all the time, there was no opportunity for socializing even if he had wanted to. Other than a couple of guys he occasionally played racquetball with at the gym, he was a loner, and he liked it. Mostly.

By following a rigid set of rules for his personal life, he kept his days running smoothly. This blip with Ophelia only proved what it cost to deviate from his usual behavior.

Again and again, he wondered what he would do if Peaches were his. Again and again, he shut down that line of thinking. Until the truth came out, speculation served no purpose.

Too late, he realized he should have changed the kid's diaper *before* giving her a bottle. Now she had sucked down the last ounce of formula and was out cold. Fortunately, Dani had already stocked most rooms in the house with diapers and wipes. Thank God for her babysitting experience. At least one of them had some exposure to infants. Otherwise, the situation would have been far worse.

Luckily for him, Peaches slept through the diaper change, even though he fumbled and cursed and struggled with the seemingly simple task. He was able to return to his room, tuck her back into the little protected corner and fall into his own bed, facedown, unconscious in seconds.

The next time he surfaced, the clock said seven. He had a hangover headache, and he hadn't even had a beer last night. Stumbling to his feet, he visited the bathroom and then moved stealthily toward Peaches's corner on the floor to check on her.

The nest was empty. Panic flooded his chest for half a second before common sense intruded. The chairs were intact. Dani must have the child.

He found them both in the kitchen. Dani had fixed a pot of coffee, God bless her, and she was sitting at the window, baby in arms, drawing pictures in the condensation on the glass.

She looked up when Nathaniel entered the room. "Good morning. It sounded like this little stinker gave you a rough night."

He winced. "You heard us?"

"I'm a light sleeper." She shrugged, her expression guarded. "I decided that if you wanted help, you would ask, so I didn't disturb you. You're a very capable man."

Pouring himself a cup of coffee and gulping it with no thought for scalding his tongue, he snorted. "Didn't feel like it last night."

"Poor Peaches. I guess she knew she was in a strange place."

"Getting stranger by the minute. Have you heard a forecast?"

She nodded glumly. "The official totals are twelve to fourteen inches so far, with more, north of the city. It's supposed to change over to freezing rain in the next couple of hours. The governor has declared a state of emergency. All roads are virtually impassable because of abandoned cars, including major interstates."

"So you're stuck with me?" He tried to smile, but the knot in his chest made it hard to breathe.

"It looks that way. But on an up note, I've already talked to my family. They're all stuck, too, except my Chattanooga sister. The storm stayed south of them. My parents have decided we'll simply postpone Christmas until at least the twenty-seventh. It's supposed to be sixty-two and sunny then."

"Welcome to winter in the South."

"Exactly."

He had no clue how to act, what to say or do. This bizarre scenario was unprecedented. Nausea swirled in his belly, and he felt light-headed.

Blaming it on the lack of sleep was less worrisome than admitting he was afraid to be trapped with Dani. Sitting there with a warm smile on her face, wearing his shirt and holding a child who was possibly his baby, she personified everything he feared, everything he had avoided for so long and so well.

He hoped like hell his unease wasn't visible. He didn't want to give in to temptation, but he sure as hell didn't want to hurt her, either.

Four

Dani cocked her head, her smile dimming as a knot of *something* settled like a rock in her stomach. Nathaniel was acting very strangely. Despite her misgivings, she forged ahead with the idea that had come to her while she waited for him to wake up. "I have a question, Nathaniel. You can say no if you want to."

As she watched, he took two steps backward, set his empty cup on the counter and shoved his hands in his pockets.

"Ask away," he said. But his gaze didn't meet hers. His body language was one big keep-off-the-grass sign.

Sighing inwardly, she nuzzled the top of the baby's head. "It's Christmas Eve," she said flatly, as if he didn't know. "And tomorrow is Christmas Day. Your condo is virtually empty of any sustenance, holiday or otherwise. I checked around online and found a small market about a mile from here that's opening up from ten to four today. If I make a grocery list, will you go shopping for us?"

His lips quirked in a reluctant smile. "That's doable."

"I'm not the greatest cook," Dani admitted. "I don't think I'd be confident preparing a turkey, even if they have any. But I could do a pot roast with all the trimmings and some kind of fancy dessert. Are you allergic to anything?"

"No." He didn't look happy.

She was even tempered as a rule, but his silence grated. "Do you have an objection to observing the holiday with good food?" The words came out more sharply than she had intended. Still, she didn't regret them.

Nathaniel sat down on a bar stool at the counter and grimaced. "My family was not as warm and fuzzy as yours, Dani. My mother was diagnosed with schizophrenia, but not until I was in high school. I don't know if you can imagine what my childhood was like."

Suddenly Dani felt small and mean. "What about your father?"

"He loved my mother in spite of everything— and he loved me, I'm sure. But he wasn't the kind of man who could keep gluing bits of our life back together and making things work. His solution was to spend all his time at the office."

"I see." In fact, she saw more than she ever had before. Nathaniel had layers upon layers, it seemed. The more she learned about him, the more it became apparent he was destined to hurt her if she let herself get too close. The man didn't want a girlfriend or a wife. In fact, he seemed to be rabidly opposed to human emotion in general.

Squashing her disappointment, she managed a light tone. "So is that yes or no to the dessert?"

Finally, she coaxed a smile from him. "I may not know how to properly observe Christmas, but I do like to eat."

"Well, there you go." For no apparent reason, Dani felt like crying. She didn't want to see Na-thaniel as a person, a man with hidden vulnerabilities. She didn't want to like or understand him anymore than she already did. Liking him led to fantasizing about a future that would never be hers. Fortunately, Nathaniel was oblivious to her turmoil.

"Your grocery store plan still doesn't help us with the baby's clothing situation, or lack thereof," he said.

Dani nodded. "I have a lead there, as well. Your poor doorman made it into work this morning, but he's bored, because clearly there's not much action in the lobby. I phoned down to him earlier with a question or two. In the process, he told me his daughter has a little girl who's a year old. He thinks they might have some hand-me-downs we can use for Peaches. And they live close enough he can walk to their apartment tonight after work."

"Do you make friends with anyone and everyone?"

His tone didn't sound as if the question was a compliment. Dani chose her words carefully. "The world can be a difficult place. We're all interconnected. I see no harm in being open to other people and experiences."

"Maybe you were a hippie flower child in another life," he muttered.

"I can go, Nathaniel," she said sharply. "You asked for my help. But if you're going to act like a horse's ass all weekend, I'd just as soon leave."

Her accusation found its mark. For a moment, Nathaniel turned icy and distant. She wanted to run from his disdain, but she held her ground. The standoff felt interminable.

Gradually, his posture softened. His chest lifted and fell in a huge sigh. "I apologize," he said. "Apparently, I'm not as good at sleep deprivation as I thought."

"You're forgiven. I know you're exhausted." Dani didn't hold grudges. Life was too short. A change of subject was in order. "I'm worried that if you get everything we need at the market, it will be too heavy to carry."

"I have an old army-surplus duffel bag. It's practically indestructible. I can load it up, cinch the top and drag it back, if necessary."

"That could work." The thought of filling Nathaniel's somewhat-sterile condo with the appealing scents of Christmas excited her.

"Is there anything else Peaches might need that I could get at the store?"

"We covered the basics last night. She's old enough to begin sampling simple foods, but since we don't know if Ophelia has given her anything yet, I'd be afraid to try. The formula will be enough for now."

"You're the expert."

"Hardly. I'm just grateful Peaches is an easy baby. I've heard stories about colic and other stuff. This situation could have been much worse."

"It *would* have been," Nathaniel said bluntly. "Without you."

She flushed. "I was an extra pair of hands, that's all."

"No," he said carefully. "It's more than that. I see it at NCT all the time. People come to you with problems and questions. You triage. You offer solutions. You give support. You're an extraordinary woman, Dani. Don't ever underestimate yourself."

With that, he turned on his heel and walked out of the room.

Dani put a hand to her hot cheek. *Wow*. That was the warmest and most personal testimonial she had ever received from her boss. And it told her he actually noticed what she did for the company. Sometimes she wondered. He became so absorbed in his work, she'd been convinced at times that he saw her as no different from a computer or the copy machine.

It was disarming to know he was watching.

Peaches had drooled all over the shoulder of Dani's shirt, which was, of course, Nathaniel's shirt. At this rate, she would have to borrow half a dozen to keep up with the baby's tendency to destroy clothing.

This was the strangest Christmas Eve Dani had ever experienced. Over the last decade, she had dated a number of men, but none of them long enough to warrant spending the holidays with their families or vice versa. The only Christmases Dani had ever known were celebrated in the bosom of her family.

Though Nathaniel's condo was a far cry from her parents' warm and welcoming home, Dani was determined to make this day memorable. For Peaches. For Nathaniel. Heck, for herself.

Someday, God willing, she would be marking the holidays in a house of her own with a husband, two as-yet-to-be-named kids and maybe a dog. *She* would be in charge of the meals and the decorations and the Santa gifts.

Maybe this odd Christmas was a testing ground. Did she have it in her to make the holiday special under these circumstances? Would Nathaniel even care?

One glance at the clock on the stove told her she had no time to spare. Presumably Nathaniel had disappeared to suit up for his foray into the winter wonderland. Dani loved playing in snow as a rule, but she didn't have the appropriate clothing, and it was too cold for the baby even if Dani had wanted to go along.

With Peaches in one arm, she quickly scanned the contents of the cabinets. They were mostly empty. One set of salt and pepper shakers. An out-of-date container of cinnamon. Half a bag of questionable flour. But at least the basics of cookware were represented. Maybe a woman had furnished the kitchen.

She found a pen and started writing. By the time Nathaniel returned carrying the big empty duffel bag, Dani had filled three pages of a notepad advertising a well-known realty company. "I hope you can read my writing," she fretted. "I'm not good at one-handed penmanship."

Nathaniel grinned. "We have these things called cell phones..."

"Well, that's true. But what if I'm changing a diaper at the exact moment you need to call me?"

He shrugged. "Then I'll wait." Even bundled from head to toe, he managed to look ruggedly handsome.

"What about eggs and bread?"

"I'll put them on top. It will be fine. Quit worrying. You should know, though, that walking a mile and back in a foot of snow won't be quick. Not to mention how long it's going to take me to find all this stuff." He waved the list in the air.

"Sorry," Dani said. "I guess I got carried away. Maybe I was making sure you didn't have to make a second trip."

"Maybe," he chuckled. He kissed the baby's cheek, his lips dangerously close to Dani's, close enough to give a woman ideas. "You girls stay out of trouble while I'm gone."

On the elevator ride down to the lobby, Nathaniel started to sweat. He'd put on clothes from his last Colorado ski trip. When he stepped outside, he was glad he had kept the heavy winter gear. As useless as it normally was in Atlanta, today it was going to come in handy.

The snow had turned into a nasty drizzle that froze on contact. Soon, he couldn't feel his cheeks. He wrapped his fleece scarf around all of his face but his eyes, and picked up the pace. It wasn't easy. Snowshoes might have been a good idea if he had owned any.

He relished the physical exertion. Despite his lack of sleep the night before, he *wanted* to push himself to the limits, anything to keep from thinking about Dani. She was his very valuable assistant, not a lover. He had to remember that, no matter how great the temptation.

He'd never seen Atlanta like this. It was a ghost town, a frozen ghost town. Occasionally, an official vehicle passed. There were a few intrepid explorers out, like himself. For the most part, though, his fellow citizens had hunkered down to wait for the snow to melt.

What did normal people do on December 24? There would be no last-minute shopping today, that's for sure. Even Amazon couldn't fulfill impulsive wishes in the midst of a blizzard. Fortunately, Nathaniel had resources Amazon didn't possess. Early this morning, he had made a couple of phone calls and arranged to get a gift for Dani. She deserved at least that much for putting up with his bizarre situation.

The small neighborhood market shone like a beacon at the end of his journey, bringing cheer to the gray, icy day. In addition to the store's normal illumination, swags of colored lights festooned the entrance.

Inside, Nathaniel grabbed a shopping cart and stripped off his outer garments. Christmas music played from overhead speakers. Oddly, it didn't irritate him as it sometimes did. When he found himself humming along with a familiar tune, he frowned and concentrated on Dani's list.

The store was mostly empty. He was able to go as slowly as he wanted, one aisle at a time, until he was confident he had fulfilled his mission.

At the checkout stand, he began to have a few tiny doubts about getting all this stuff back to the condo. No matter. He'd told Dani it might take a while.

The store manager rang up the purchases.

"You're a brave man," he said. "Must have a woman at home ready to cook."

"Something like that."

When the last item was scanned, Nathaniel handed over his credit card and began loading the canvas duffel, putting the canned goods on the bottom. The manager looked to be in his late forties and bore a passing resemblance to Santa Claus. He was dressed in overalls and a red flannel shirt, probably not his usual work attire.

The older man began grouping smaller items and tying them into plastic bags to make them easier to stuff in the duffel. "You got a tree already?" he asked.

Nathaniel shook his head. "No. I don't usually decorate. It's a lot of trouble."

The Santa look-alike frowned. "Then you should take one of those small live trees. On the house. They'll be useless to me by Monday. For that matter, I'll throw in a stand and several strands of lights. Might as well. I'll be stuck with that whole display seventy-five percent off. I'd rather you and your lady friend enjoy them."

"Oh, but I—"

The manager interrupted, "I know, I know.

You're walking. I get it. My son, Toby, is in the back unloading pallets. Do you know how hard it is for a seventeen-year-old boy to be snowed in the day before Christmas? The kid needs some exercise. He's driving me and his mom crazy. Let him walk back and carry the tree for you."

"It's a long way," Nathaniel protested.

"Won't matter." The man punched in a message on his cell phone. "He's on his way."

Moments later the kid appeared. Six foot four at least, with shoulders that told Nathaniel he probably played football. The teenager was visibly eager, chomping at the bit to get outside. "Happy to help, sir," he said, beaming at Nathaniel. "Which tree would you like?"

Nathaniel wanted to say *forget it*, but in his gut he knew Dani would love having a tree. "Any of them." Good grief.

The manager grimaced. "Sorry we don't have ornaments."

"Believe me," Nathaniel said, "it's okay."

The trip back to the condo was surprisingly entertaining. Nathaniel dragged the heavy duffel bag along behind him, occasionally changing arms when his shoulder protested. "So tell me, Toby, do you work at the store on a regular basis?"

"When I'm not practicing football or basketball or out with my girl."

Toby had the four-foot, live tree—in a plastic stand—balanced on one shoulder. In his other hand, he carried Dani's precious eggs, a loaf of bread and the strands of lights. The teenager wasn't even breathing hard, nor was he wearing gloves. Nathaniel, probably only fifteen years his senior, felt like an old man trying to keep up.

"Have you been dating this girl for a while?"

"A year and a half, sir. We have plans to go to college together and get married when we graduate."

"Your parents are okay with that?"

"Oh, yeah. They adore Kimberly. Her parents have been married almost as long as mine. Mom always told me to look at a girl's family. That way you know what's important to her, and you can decide if you're compatible."

The young man's casual confidence rattled Nathaniel. Was this what happened when you grew up with actual parental guidance? Surely this kid was far too young to know what he wanted out of life. Then again, Nathaniel wasn't qualified to weigh in on interpersonal relationships, not by a long shot.

Toby used the next twenty minutes to bend Nathaniel's ear about everything from his interest in NASCAR racing to his amazing girlfriend to the Central America trip he and his youth group were going to make during the summer.

Nathaniel listened with half an ear, wondering if he himself had ever been as passionate and excited about life as this young man. For Nathaniel, every goal had been about getting out on his own and proving himself *without* his parents. Yet here was an all-American kid who actually enjoyed his life.

Even Toby tired after the first half mile. When they stopped to catch their breath, Toby set the tree and his packages carefully on the ground and rolled his shoulders. He even put on a pair of gloves.

Nathaniel hid a grin. He did remember what it was like to be seventeen and driven by testosterone. Of course, with Dani in his home, those feelings were pretty much the same right now. He didn't feel the need to flex his muscles, but on the other hand, he *had* made a long trek through knee-deep ice and snow to bring home provisions. Maybe this was the twenty-first-century equivalent of slaying a wild animal and dragging it back to the cave.

Toby blew on his hands and bounced from one foot to the other. "What about you, Mr. Winston. Do you have any kids?"

For some reason, the question caught Nathaniel completely off guard. "Um, no…"

Toby grinned. "You don't sound too sure."

"I'm sure," Nathaniel said firmly. "Come on. Let's get going before we freeze to death."

At the condo, Dani buzzed them in and welcomed them at the door. The way her face lit up when she saw the scrawny little tree gave Nathaniel a warm fuzzy feeling that was scary as hell.

"This is Toby," Nathaniel said. "His dad manages the market. Toby got drafted to help me get back with all of this."

Dani beamed at the teenager, baby Peaches on her hip. "Thank you *so* much, Toby. Here, wait." She reached into her purse on the table in the foyer and pulled out a twenty-dollar bill. "Merry Christmas."

The boy's cheeks reddened even more than they had from the cold. Dani's smile could melt a snowman at fifty paces. "Merry Christmas, ma'am. Happy to do it."

"Will you stay long enough for me to make some hot chocolate?" Dani asked.

Toby grimaced. "Wish I could, but I'd better get back to the store. Your baby is cute." Peaches flirted with him unashamedly.

Dani blinked. "Oh, well, she's not mine, but thanks."

Toby shot Nathaniel a raised-eyebrow look. The baby wasn't Dani's, and Nathaniel had said he didn't have kids. No wonder the boy was confused.

Nathaniel decided to hurry the goodbyes along. "Too bad you can't stay. Thanks for your help. Tell your father thanks, too. Merry Christmas."

When the door closed behind the teenager, an awkward silence fell, one that weighed a thousand pounds. Nathaniel cleared his throat. "I got a tree," he said.

Dani nodded, eyes wide, cheeks flushed. "I see that."

"I thought you'd like it, it being Christmas Eve and all." He didn't tell her it wasn't his idea.

"I think it's wonderful," Dani said softly. She went up on tiptoe and kissed his cheek, so quickly he barely felt it. "Thank you, Nathaniel." She paused. "If you don't mind taking the baby, I'll start putting the groceries away. Would you like something warm to drink? I have a fresh pot of coffee brewing."

"Give me a minute first," he said gruffly. "I need a shower and different clothes."

Dani regretted the kiss as soon as she did it. She wasn't sure what had come over her except that she had been so darned touched by Nathaniel's effort. Toby had helped significantly, but still...

She suspected she had either shocked her boss or made him extremely uncomfortable or both. She came from a very affectionate family. For a moment, she had forgotten where she was. It was a mistake she wouldn't repeat. Nathaniel had disappeared so fast, he probably left a trail of steam.

Before Toby departed, the two men had hefted

the full-to-the-brim canvas duffel onto the granite-topped kitchen island. Even with Peaches on one hip, Dani was able to begin putting cans and dry goods into the cupboard. She often enjoyed watching cooking shows on cable, but she didn't consider herself a pro. Something about Christmas Eve, though, gave her a tingling sense of anticipation for the dinner to come.

"Here's the thing," she whispered to Peaches. "It would be super helpful if you would take a nice long nap. Nathaniel needs one, too, and I have a ton of cooking to do." The little girl gazed up at her, fist in mouth. She didn't look at all sleepy.

"Okay, fine. Stay awake. But Santa doesn't visit cranky children, now does he?"

After half an hour, Nathaniel still hadn't appeared. Was he avoiding her? If they were to eat at a decent hour, she needed to get the roast in the oven and start on the pecan pie. For Christmas morning, she had planned a coffee cake with streusel topping and mimosas. Christmas lunch would consist of open-faced beef sandwiches with a cranberry salad.

Without the internet, she would have been lost.

Her phone was her lifeline. It helped that Nathaniel kept a drawer full of extra charging cords. Impromptu travel with literally nothing except her purse was not the easiest thing in the world.

When four thirty rolled around, she decided to go in search of her missing boss. She found him facedown on his mattress, sound asleep. Poor man. She knew he wouldn't have left her to handle everything on purpose.

He was bare from the waist up, his tan evidence of holidays spent in tropical climates. His shoulders and back were smoothly muscled. The pair of navy knit pants he had pulled on rode low on his narrow hips.

This was what Nathaniel Winston would look like on lazy Saturday mornings before he climbed out of bed. *Or maybe he sleeps in the nude, Dani. He can't very well do that with his executive assistant and a baby in the house.*

Her cheeks hot, she debated her course of action. Peaches took it out of her hands. The little girl chortled loudly. Nathaniel shot straight up in bed, wild-eyed. "What's wrong?" He scraped his hands through his hair.

"Nothing," Dani said quickly. "Sorry to wake

you. But I need to start dinner, and I can only do so much one-handed. I thought Peaches would be asleep by now, but she obviously knows it's Christmas Eve, and she's too excited to close her eyes."

Nathaniel didn't seem amused by her whimsy. "Let me have her. We'll play in the den and stay out of your way."

"How thoughtful," she said, deadpan.

His sharp look questioned her sincerity, and rightly so. It didn't take a genius to see that Nathaniel wanted to avoid Dani as much as possible. Fine. She didn't need him in the kitchen getting underfoot anyway.

Fortunately, her ambitious Christmas Eve dinner menu consumed her attention for most of the subsequent hour. Once she had seared the roast and tucked it in a deep pan flanked with carrots and potatoes, she put the pie together and popped the sweet treat in the oven with the meat, very glad both dishes cooked at the same temperature.

The condo had a small dining room just off the kitchen. Inside a modern-looking buffet, Dani found navy placemats that matched the navy-and-cream stoneware in the kitchen cabinets. It frustrated her not to have the trappings of holiday colors or even a store-bought poinsettia. Even a couple of red candles would have been nice.

That was the problem with bachelors. They didn't know how to set a scene anywhere but in the bedroom.

Oops. Thinking about Nathaniel and bedrooms was bad mojo. She was already in trouble for her innocent thank-you kiss. Best not to let him see that she was curious enough and attracted enough to be fascinated by thoughts of his private life.

Which brought her directly back to Peaches and Ophelia. Damn Nathaniel's mystery woman. How had she found the chutzpah to pull off such an outrageous stunt?

Brooding over the baby's lack of a proper Christmas didn't help matters. Best to concentrate on what she could control. The only thing left was to put together a spinach-and-almond salad and prepare a light dressing. Serving pieces were ready. She and Nathaniel could take turns holding the baby during dinner, if necessary.

The roast and pecan pie had to cook for thirty more minutes. Plenty of time to put the Christmas tree in the den and decorate it. That meant running into Nathaniel again, but at least he had put on a shirt before he left his bedroom.

She knew that only because he had made a quick appearance in the kitchen earlier to grab coffee. Neither of them was dressed for a formal Christmas Eve meal. She supposed he had kept his appearance very casual in light of her predicament.

Wistfully, she imagined what it would be like if they were actually dating. She might find herself wearing a very special, sexy dress, knowing, or at least hoping, that Nathaniel would remove it at the end of the evening.

After her boss's chilly reception earlier, it took a measure of courage to intrude on his privacy. But the den was arguably the best place for the tree, and this designer condo needed a punch of color and light, tonight of all nights.

Nathaniel didn't look up when she entered the den dragging the tree along behind her. The fir had lost a significant percentage of its needles en route from the store, but it was still presentable. With the heavy plastic base already attached, all Dani would have to do was add some water tonight before going to bed. After all, the tree would stand guard beside the fireplace barely twenty-four hours before the lord of the manor tossed it out. She was pretty sure she knew Nathaniel that well.

Without speaking, she unboxed the tiny lights and began twining them around the tree, attaching one strand to the next. Still, Nathaniel didn't acknowledge her presence. Peaches sat on his knee, trying to get one of his shirt buttons in her mouth. Nathaniel held her firmly, but his attention was on the television. He flipped channels rapidly, presumably checking the football scores.

When she finished the tree and plugged it in, she expected at least a token comment. Her boss was mute. He had to have noticed the cheerful Christmas tree. It upped the cozy factor of the den tenfold. But maybe Nathaniel just didn't care. Stubborn, gorgeous man. She didn't know whether she wanted to kiss him or smack him.

Subdued and disappointed, she tweaked a branch and turned to walk out of the room. "Dinner in twenty minutes," she said over her shoulder.

"Wait, Dani," he said.

She turned around, bracing herself for criticism. "What?"

He lifted a shoulder and let it fall. "I don't mind the tree. But don't expect too much from me. This holiday stuff isn't my thing."

Five

A man knew when he was being an ass. Dani walked out on him without another word. Nathaniel was fully cognizant that he was exhibiting every characteristic of a bad host. The stupid Christmas tree was charming. And festive. Even Peaches cooed when she saw it. So why had he deliberately downplayed Dani's efforts?

Why were the aromas wafting from the kitchen both tantalizing and unsettling? He didn't want his condo to smell like Christmas. He didn't want a tree. He didn't want Dani.

What a liar you are. His libido was more honest than he.

In barely twenty-four hours, Dani had transformed Nathaniel's hideout from the world into a warm, holiday-scented, incredibly appealing home. How she had done it so quickly and so well, he couldn't exactly say. It was more than the groceries and the tree, though he couldn't put his finger on what was so different with her here.

Maybe it was the baby. Everyone knew that babies were precious and cute. Perhaps little Peaches was bachelor kryptonite. He sniffed her hair, wondering for the millionth time if he was her biological father. Shouldn't he be able to tell instinctively? Wasn't there some sort of parental bonding moment when all became clear?

If there was, he hadn't experienced it yet.

Dani didn't bother calling him to dinner. His phone dinged with a blunt, unemotional text. It's ready...

Standing up with a sigh, he took the baby to the tree. "Do you like it?" he asked softly. "It's supposed to have ornaments, but I don't have a single one."

The baby reached out to grab the lights. She'd probably chew the cord in two if he let her. Those bottom teeth had to be poking through soon. "No touching," he warned, nuzzling the top of her head with his chin. "We'd better go wash up for dinner before Dani loses patience with us."

The kitchen was filled with steam, delightful smells and a woman who resembled his efficient executive assistant, but in this setting looked more like a wife. The knot in his stomach grew.

Dani glared at him, clearly upset that he hadn't appreciated her efforts with the tree.

"Smells wonderful," he said, hoping to win a few points with genuine appreciation for her culinary efforts.

"We're eating in the dining room," she said, her tone frosty. "We may as well serve our plates in here. That way things won't get cold. I took the liberty of opening a bottle of wine. Let me have the baby. After you fix your plate, I'll do mine. There's plenty, but save room for dessert."

The solid meat-and-potatoes meal reminded him of something his grandmother might have prepared. His mother had grown up in her aunt's home, an orphan by the age of eight. But Nathaniel had substantial memories of his paternal grandmother. She had come over from Italy and spoke heavily accented English. Her cooking had been sublime.

He piled food onto his plate unapologetically. After his marathon trip in the snow today, a few extra calories were neither here nor there. Once he had set his plate in the dining room, he took the baby back. "Your turn, Madam Chef," he said lightly. To his surprise, Dani disappeared and came back lugging the Fraser fir—stand, lights and all.

"That's the advantage of a small tree," she said smugly. "They're sort of portable."

She plugged in the lights and sat down. At the last moment, she took her phone from her pocket and cued up Christmas music. Soon, they were eating in silence, save for the holiday tunes playing softly in the background.

With every bite Nathaniel took, his stomach tightened. The food was spectacular. The baby behaved. It was something else, something powerful and dangerous that stole his appetite and tightened his throat.

In this room, here and now, was everything he had never had, everything he told himself he didn't need. Family time. Cozy holidays. A beautiful, capable woman willing to work at his side to create a home.

He forced himself to clear his plate in deference to Dani's efforts on his behalf. Two glasses of wine didn't still his unease. They chatted lazily during the meal about the weather and the bowl games and whether the thaw would start Monday or wait until Tuesday.

Eventually, the baby fell asleep in Dani's arms. The two females were flushed and beautiful, Madonna and child.

"I feel terrible about this," Dani said suddenly, her expression troubled.

"About what?" There was no way she could have read his mind.

"About Peaches's first Christmas. She should have a stocking and leave cookies for Santa. That's how it's done, or so I'm told. Her mother's selfish behavior is robbing her of a special occasion."

Nathaniel shook his head. "As far as that baby's concerned, today might as well be April Fools'. The kid doesn't know the difference."

"*I* know," Dani said stubbornly.

"There's nothing we can do about it."

"If this was *Little House on the Prairie*, I'd make her a pinafore out of a flour sack, and you'd carve her a toy train with your pocketknife."

Even in the midst of his turmoil, he was amused. "I don't own a pocketknife."

"Well, I should have bought you one for Christmas."

An awkward silence fell. Nathaniel wished he was holding the baby. Peaches was a helpful decoy and a place to focus his attention.

In a few hours, it would be Christmas Day. If this was how Dani did Christmas Eve, what did she have up her sleeve for the following morning?

For the briefest of moments, he caught a flash of the two of them in bed, laughing, the baby between them. At the table eating breakfast. In front of the tree, opening presents. Panic shot through him with the force of an erupting geyser.

"This isn't real," he said, concealing his desperation beneath a veneer of calm.

Dani looked at him with a frown. "What's not real? The food? The baby? The tree? I'm confused."

He stood up to pace, tossing his napkin on the table. "We need to talk, Dani."

Her face went white, and she clutched the baby closer. "Go right ahead. Say what you have to say."

"*None* of this is real," he said doggedly. "We're not a family. This isn't a Norman Rockwell Christmas Eve. You and I are business associates. Peaches being with me is a big misunderstanding."

"I don't understand why you're so upset," Dani said quietly. She watched him with big blue eyes that saw far more than he wanted her to see.

Seeking to temper his anxiety and his distress, he sucked in a huge breath and turned his back for a moment on the sight of Dani and the baby sitting at his elegant mahogany table. The blizzard was to blame for all of this. All he had to do was remember that life would get back to normal soon.

He swung back around and sighed. "My father lost his company in his midfifties."

Dani blinked. "He did?"

Nathaniel nodded jerkily. "I told you my mother was not diagnosed until I was in high school. The episode that triggered her hospitalization was so severe she suffered a massive break from reality."

"That must have been terrifying for you and your dad."

"My father protected her as best he could all those years, but now she was institutionalized with little hope of returning home. It crushed him. He couldn't or wouldn't confide in me. Maybe he thought I was too young. The stress affected his health. Eventually, he found solace in the arms of a woman who worked for him. It didn't last long. Still, the damage was done. The employee filed a sexual harassment lawsuit, including charges for mental pain and anguish. A court awarded her a huge settlement, and my father had to liquidate the company to meet his obligations."

Nathaniel expected some response from Dani, any response. She stared at him blankly, as if nothing he had said made sense.

The silence grew—with it, the certainty he had ripped apart something fragile and wonderful. Dani's long-lashed blue eyes shone with tears. To her credit, she blinked them back successfully.

She bit her lip, her pallor marked. "Let me be sure I understand. This lecture you're giving me is because I cooked dinner and dared to acknowledge that tonight is Christmas Eve? Based on that, you're afraid I'm going to sue you and take away your livelihood? Have I got it, Nathaniel? Is that what you're telling me?"

"You're making me sound like a lunatic," he said sullenly.

Dani jumped to her feet, glaring at him, and headed for the door. Her chin wobbled ever so slightly. "No," she said, her voice tight with hurt. "You're doing a fine job of that all on your own. The thing is, Nathaniel, you're not a Scrooge at all. You're something far worse. Scrooge had a change of heart in his life. You don't have a heart at all. You're a machine. A cardboard figure of a man, a coward. I hope you choke on your pie."

If she had stormed out of the room, he might have found the energy to fight back. Instead, her icy, dignified departure warned him to let her go. It was Christmas Eve. The woman who had helped him with his baby crisis and done her best to create a bit of holiday joy in the midst of a snowstorm was insulted and pained beyond words, and it was his fault.

He should have handled things better. Nothing he said was a lie. But what he had failed to mention was how much it hurt to see what his life might have been like if he hadn't learned from his father's weakness.

Nathaniel didn't want to be weak. He didn't want the responsibility of a spouse and children. His life had been rumbling along just fine. Why in the devil had he let himself fall prey to feelings that were nothing more than syrupy commercialism?

Holiday music and Christmas lights and good food were nothing more than a Band-Aid covering the world's ills. Come Monday, everyone's life would be as good or as bad as it ever was. Nathaniel was guided by reason and pragmatism. Those qualities in his leadership style had helped make New Century Tech prosper.

Doggedly, he ignored the sick lump of dread in his stomach. He went to the kitchen, cut a piece of the beautiful pecan pie, topped it with a swirl of whipped cream and returned to the dining room to eat his dessert in solitary splendor. After several minutes, he placed his fork on the empty plate and rested his elbows on the table, head in his hands.

Damn it, the pie was good. Downright amazing. The pecans had a crunchy glaze and the filling was sweet but not too sweet. If you wanted to know what happiness and love tasted like, this was it.

The condo was as quiet as a winter snowfall. Nathaniel had spent at least half a dozen December 24ths alone during his adult life, maybe a few more. But tonight—this very moment—was the first time he had ever *noticed* something was missing on Christmas Eve.

His outburst drained him. Dani's stricken response excoriated him. He felt raw, his emotions exposed for all the world to see. It wouldn't have mattered so much except that he valued Dani's good opinion.

Moving quietly, he cleared the table and set about cleaning up the kitchen. It was only fair. He hadn't helped with meal preparations. Truthfully, though, the reason for his efforts was more about delaying consequences than it was having a tidy home.

His brain whirred, jumping from thought to thought like a hound dog chasing butterflies in a meadow. What had he done? For that matter, what was he doing now? If Peaches were really his daughter, what did the future hold for him?

In forty-five minutes, every pot and pan and plate and bowl was out of sight. Countertops gleamed. It was easy enough to restore a kitchen to its original state. Unfortunately, the harsh words he had served Dani were far more difficult to put back in the box.

First things first. He picked up his phone and sent a text.

It's late. I'm coming to your room to get Peaches.

Dani's response was quick and terse.

No. She's asleep. You had her last night. My turn.

Nathaniel sent two more texts insisting that he be the one to deal with the baby, but there was no response at all. Either Dani had turned off her phone, or she was ignoring him. He couldn't bring himself to knock on her door. She deserved her privacy.

After half-heartedly watching TV for a couple of hours, he headed to his own room, intending to read. He'd bought the latest medical thriller by an author he admired. That should distract him from his jumbled thoughts.

Unfortunately, all he could focus on was the image of Dani. By now he had memorized everything about her. The low, husky music of her laugh. The way her blue eyes changed from light and sparkly to navy and mysterious. The graceful way she moved.

As the night waned, he dozed only in snatches. The silence in the house became oppressive. Was Dani okay? Was Peaches? Were both females sound asleep? He'd never experienced the wakefulness of being responsible for another human being.

Actually, that wasn't true. Long ago, during a time he tried to forget, this same stomach-curling worry had been his from time to time. Whenever his father had gone out of town on business, he always reminded Nathaniel to *keep an eye on your mother.*

Nathaniel had never really understood what he was watching out for. He only knew that his mother was not like his friends' moms. Those women baked cookies and sat on the bleachers at T-ball games. Nathaniel's mother mostly ignored him. When she did focus on his hapless self, her tendency was to smother him with adoration that held a marked tinge of frantic desperation and mania.

As much as he had craved her attention as a boy, he learned early on that it was better for the family dynamic when she didn't notice him.

His thoughts drifted back to Dani. She was warm and nurturing and so completely natural with Peaches. Not one echo of disapproval or reluctance marked the way she related to the baby. Even if she thought Nathaniel was a cold bastard for ignoring his own child up until now, she never voiced her concern. He had no idea if she believed him or not when he said the infant wasn't his.

What if he were wrong?

The mental struggles kept on coming. In the wee hours of Christmas morning, Nathaniel faced an unpalatable truth—the real reason he had created such an unfortunate scene at dinner.

For months now, he had been deeply attracted to his executive assistant. The only way he had been able to manage his unfortunate response to her was to pretend she was part of the office furnishings. Maintaining the status quo meant he was the boss and Dani an extremely valued employee.

The blizzard, along with Ophelia's dramatic stunt, had upset the balance in Nathaniel's life. At this point, he doubted whether the tide could be turned again. Dani was funny, compassionate...a *real*, breathing woman living beneath his roof. He liked her scent and the messy knot she fashioned to keep her hair out of her face. He loved the way her generous curves filled out his boring dress shirts.

Seeing her in his clothes was gut-level sexy. Like a film star in a magazine caught on camera in her own backyard, Dani was just Dani. No artifice. No mask to hide behind. No attempt to impress.

Nathaniel was very much afraid he was infatuated with her, maybe worse.

As he lay there in the dark, battling emotions he had kept locked away for so long, his chest ached and his eyes burned. Damn Ophelia. Damn the storm. If things hadn't gotten all jacked up, perhaps he could gradually have tested the waters with Dani.

Instead, here they were, thrust together in a faux environment. His sex hardened and his breathing grew ragged. What would it be like to take her here in his bed? Did she even have a boyfriend?

It stunned him to realize he didn't know the answer to that question. In the midst of his fantasies lay the grim realization he was probably the last person on the planet to whom Dani Meadows would turn for a relationship.

In little more than a week, they would both be back at New Century Tech, hard at work, each easing into familiar roles. Could he bear it? After having her here, just down the hall, would he be able to treat her like an employee again?

At 3:00 a.m., he climbed out of bed. He was only torturing himself by trying to sleep. In his sock feet, he tiptoed down the hall and listened at the guest room door. Not a sound emanated from within, though a tiny strip of light showed underneath the door.

He tapped quietly. "Dani. Are you awake?"

No answer. Any one of a number of possibilities came to mind. Dani might have fallen asleep exhausted and left a light on unintentionally.

Or perhaps it was on so she could check the baby easily.

He shouldn't open the door. Every rule or law of hospitality expressly forbade it. Not to mention the fact that he and Dani had parted on angry terms.

Nathaniel turned the knob anyway.

The room was empty.

He stood there in the middle of the expensive plush carpet with his mouth agape. The bathroom door was open. No sense peering in there. Dani would have been talking to the baby if they were in residence. He liked how she communicated with the kid as if Peaches could understand every word.

Clearly, Dani had managed to slip quietly past Nathaniel's bedroom without him hearing a single thing.

Undaunted in his quest, he did an about-face and headed for the den. There he found a scene that gripped his heart and wouldn't let go.

Somehow, maybe while the baby slept, Dani had retrieved the small tree from the dining room and returned it to the place of honor beside the dancing orange and yellow flames. A simple cotton afghan was spread at the base of the tree. The baby slept peacefully on her tummy, one fist curled against her cheek.

Dani wasn't asleep at all. She sat on the stone hearth, elbows on her knees, fingers steepled beneath her chin. Wearing only his shirt that reached almost to her knees, she was barelegged and gorgeous. The misery on her face made his chest hurt.

He took the end of the sofa nearest the fireplace and leaned forward to face her. "I'm sorry," he said.

"No, you're not." Dani's cold certainty was worse than her anger. "You meant every word you said. The only reason you have any regrets now is because we're stuck with each other for at least another thirty-six hours, maybe more."

"Will you cut me some slack?" he pleaded.

"Why? Why should I?"

Who knew that blue eyes could freeze a man? He swallowed. "I don't know if I can explain."

"Try me." Perhaps she wasn't completely calm. She jumped to her feet and wrapped her arms around her waist, standing beside their small, fragrant Christmas tree and staring at it intently as if it had the power to provide answers to difficult questions.

She was so beautiful and yet so far away. *He* had put that emotional distance between them. Because he was scared. "Look at me, Dani." He stood as well, but he didn't pace. This was too important.

Slowly, she turned to face him. He couldn't read her expression. The woman who was usually open and without artifice had locked her emotions in a deep freeze. "You're the boss," she quipped, her tone deliberately inflammatory.

"This isn't easy for me," he said. The words felt like sand in his throat.

That chin wobble thing happened again. Dani's jaw worked as if she were trying not to cry. "Today is the worst Christmas I've ever had," she whispered. "And that's counting the one when my mom was in the hospital with pneumonia and my father burned the turkey. So don't talk to me about easy."

He bowed his head, tormented by guilt, wracked by indecision. No bolt of divine intervention came to save him. With a deep ragged breath, he managed to look at her straight on without flinching. "I'm becoming obsessed with you, Dani…and that scares the hell out of me. I don't know what to do."

"You probably ate too much," she taunted. "Indigestion passes. Grab an antacid. You'll be fine."

"Don't be flip," he growled. "I'm serious. All I can think about is kissing you to see where it takes us."

As it had earlier in the dining room, every scrap of color drained from Dani's face, leaving her pale. "You don't want to kiss me, not really. You think I'll ruin your life."

"Of course I want to kiss you, but that *won't* be the end of it. You're in my head, damn it. And in my gut. I can't sleep." He paused, his forehead damp and his hands clammy. In desperation, he said the one thing that a woman like Dani might respond to favorably. "I need you, Dani. Badly."

Almost in slow motion, he reached out and took her hand in his. She looked at him with an expression that was three parts fear and one part the same burning curiosity tearing him apart. If she had shown the slightest resistance, he would have stopped instantly.

Instead, she took a step toward him. "Nathaniel." The way she said his name, husky and sweet, was his undoing. He dragged her against his chest and held her so tightly she laughed softly.

"I have to breathe," she said.

Releasing her a millimeter, he sighed. "I'll breathe for both of us." He rested his chin on top of her head, feeling the silky, caramel-taffy waves tickle his middle-of-the-night beard. "Tell me to stop," he pleaded hoarsely.

"I won't." She licked the pulse beating at the base of his throat. "But I won't be accused of seduction, though. If we do this, it's all on you, *Mr.* Winston. Maybe you should think long and hard before you do something you'll regret."

Her schoolmarmish admonishment only made him more desperate. How could she stand there and be so cool? "I'm already long and hard," he complained. "That's what I'm trying to tell you."

Dani felt ill. For months and months, she had wondered what it would be like to have Nathaniel look at her the way a man looks at a woman he desires. Well, now she knew. And it wasn't good.

Her boss didn't *want* to want her. Somehow that was a thousand times worse than the strict professionalism he showed her in their working relationship.

It took everything she had to pull away from him and back up when all she wanted to do was rip off his clothes. "I'm serious, Nathaniel. Do we have a physical spark—yes, but you're giving me mixed signals. Heaven knows that might be the understatement of the year. I'm a grown woman. I have needs, too. We're snowed in together with nothing to distract us. It stands to reason we might feel *something*. That doesn't mean we have to act on it."

"I said I was sorry for earlier." His gaze was stormy and hot with male intent.

"Sorry, maybe. But you spoke the truth. What could possibly induce me to do something so reckless and self-destructive?"

Reeling her in for a second time, he smoothed stray hairs from her cheek and tucked them behind her ear, his smile lopsided. The touch of his fingertips on her hot skin undid her. Like a foolish Victorian maiden made to swoon by pretty words and innocent caresses, she melted into his embrace.

As kisses went, it was world-class. Despite his

professed conflicted emotions, Nathaniel was now totally in control, completely confident. He held her without a sign of awkwardness, as though the two of them had been intimate for weeks and months.

To his credit, he coaxed rather than insisted. The first kiss was soft and warm and exploratory. His taste was sinful and decadent. Dani's hands clung to his shoulders as if she were about to go down with the *Titanic*. Her heart beat so loudly in her ears, she wondered if he noticed.

One of his arms held her firmly against his chest. The other hand tangled in her hair and loosened the rubber band that was her only claim to style. Now her hair tumbled onto her shoulders. She had washed it at bedtime. It was still damp.

Nathaniel shuddered and buried his face in the curve of her neck. "You smell like apple pie," he muttered.

"It's the shampoo in your guest bathroom," she said primly. One part of her brain couldn't believe this was actually happening.

"Please tell me I'm not making a fool of myself, Dani."

She shook her head, finally brave enough to stroke the silky hair at the back of his neck. "You're a lot of things, Nathaniel Winston. But never a fool."

He pulled back and stared into her eyes. "Do you want me? Do you want this? Be honest, please."

Taking his face between her hands, she managed a smile. "I've never wanted anything more." She paused, biting her lip.

"What?" he asked sharply.

His frown alarmed her. "I'm on the Pill, but I need you to wear protection."

"Of course."

A dark red flush spread from his throat to his hairline. She had either embarrassed him or angered him. "I'm not the kind of woman who takes chances," she said, "all evidence to the contrary."

"Of course not," he said. "But you need to believe me when I say I took no chances with Ophelia. It might have been a one-night stand, but I'm not suicidal. I used condoms. If Peaches is mine, it was conception that defied the odds."

The baby in question slept peacefully at their

feet, the lights on the little tree casting colored shadows on her small body.

Dani sighed. "I believe you. Accidents happen, though."

He gripped her wrist, forcing her attention away from the child and back to him. "I'll get condoms," he said. "Don't move."

Nodding jerkily, she forced a smile. "Hurry."

When she was alone again, Dani blinked and sank to her knees on the rug. "Oh, Peaches. What have I done?"

Six

For one wild moment, Dani started to scoop up the baby. It wouldn't be hard to prevent herself from crossing a monumental line in the sand. All she had to do was pretend Peaches had awakened on her own. Babies did that all the time.

Her hand hovered over the downy head for what seemed like forever. Nerves sent her stomach into a free fall and then whooshed it back up again. *Oh, God, am I insane?* Nathaniel Winston was going to break her heart.

"Having second thoughts?"

The masculine voice startled her so badly, she lost her balance and sat down hard on her butt. "I didn't expect you back so soon."

He stared at her strangely. "My bedroom is two doors away. How long did you think it would take?"

"Oh." Suddenly, her nerves returned full force. Nathaniel was a sophisticated, highly sexual man. Dani was completely out of her depth. She swallowed hard. "When I fantasized about this, I was wearing my best panties and a sexy negligee."

His jaw dropped. "You fantasized about me?"

"Well, of course. You're you. Don't you ever look in a mirror?"

"That's ridiculous."

Against all odds, she had gained a temporary advantage. She stuck out her hand. "Help me up, please." When his hard, warm palm took hers, male fingers clasping smaller female ones, she exhaled shakily. "I didn't change my mind."

"Thank God."

Nathaniel scooped her up in his arms and carried her the few steps to the sofa. He deposited her on her back and began unbuttoning the borrowed shirt she wore. Dani had already rinsed out her only set of underwear in preparation for wearing it again the following day. Consequently, she was completely naked underneath.

When Nathaniel realized that pertinent fact, he froze for several seconds. Then he laid back the two sides of the shirt and studied her raptly. "Merry Christmas to me," he muttered, his eyes glazed with unmistakable hunger.

Dani had the strongest urge to reach for the afghan and cover herself. Her breasts were on the large side. Her tummy wasn't completely flat. The women in her family loved to cook and it showed. "Turn off the lamp," she begged. "We'll still have the tree."

Nathaniel shook his head slowly. "No. I want to see everything."

Reverently, he put a hand on one breast, cupping her fullness with his fingers.

Dani flinched instinctively. She wanted to dive into sex without thinking, letting madness take control. Instead, Nathaniel seemed prepared to savor the moment.

She reached for the hem of his shirt, trying to lift it over his head. "We should hurry," she said. "Before the baby wakes up."

Nathaniel grabbed her wrist. "Not so fast. I want to look at you."

Apparently, he meant that quite literally. For the longest time, he simply stared. Beneath his intense regard, the tips of her breasts pebbled and ached. Gooseflesh broke out all over her body, though the room was plenty warm.

"Nathaniel…" She trailed off, not sure what she wanted to say.

His gaze met hers. "What?" His pupils were dilated.

"You're embarrassing me."

A tiny frown creased the real estate between his eyebrows. "Why? You're exquisite. A man could lose himself for hours doing nothing more than this." But at last, he released her breast and placed his hand, palm flat, on her abdomen. "I want to spend all night learning what you like… what you want."

"We don't have all night." It was true. They'd be lucky to have half an hour. Why was Nathaniel wasting time? She rested her fingertips on his taut thigh. "I want you naked. That's my Christmas wish right now. Come to me, Nathaniel."

Her urgent plea got through to him. With one rueful glance at the sleeping baby, he stood and ripped his shirt over his head.

The man was beautiful. There was no other way to describe it. Broad shoulders, a dusting of dark hair on his tautly muscled chest, bronzed skin. When he dragged the soft cotton pants down his legs and kicked them away, his erection sprang free, tall and thick and ready for action.

Oh, my.

He knelt beside the sofa and touched her upper thigh. "Let me pleasure you, sweet Dani. I want to hear you scream my name."

What followed next was an erotic assault on her senses. He caressed and teased and aroused her until she was half-mad with wanting him and completely blind to all the reasons she shouldn't. Dani had been with only two men. One was a long-term relationship in her early twenties, one that didn't work out. The second was a mistake born of loneliness and the conviction that life was passing her by.

Now here was Nathaniel. Not long-term. Definitely a mistake.

How could a woman leap into disaster and not even care? Turned out, it was easy. Too easy. All she had to do was close her eyes and pretend that Nathaniel was her happily-ever-after. That's what women did, right? Weave fantasies?

Unfortunately, Nathaniel wasn't in a mood to appease her fairy tales. At last, he stood again, this time coming down on top of her and moving between her thighs. "Open your eyes, Dani. This is me you're hiding from. I won't have it. Open your eyes."

Holding Nathaniel's gaze while he slid deep into her body shattered her. He witnessed every nuance of her reaction, including the slight wince when he pressed as far as he could go, thrust irrevocably at the mouth of her womb.

Dani shuddered and panted. It was too much and not enough. He filled her almost uncomfortably. She was tense and frightened—not of Nathaniel, but of her own wildly careening emotions.

She turned her head, watching the dancing flames that somehow had found their way into her body and were roasting her alive.

Her lover grasped her chin and turned her

head to face him. His gaze was fierce. "If you wanted to change your mind, all you had to do was say so."

Shocked to the tips of her bare toes, she saw that she had hurt him. "Oh, Nathaniel, no. It's not that. I want you, I do." She linked her arms around his neck and canted her hips, allowing him to steal one more millimeter.

He kissed her roughly, his tongue tangling with hers. "Then why do you keep escaping in your head?" He nibbled the sensitive flesh below her ear and raked her collarbone with sharp teeth.

Dani moaned. "I'm scared. You make me crazy." She was afraid to come, terrified that she would shatter into a million jagged pieces and never be the same again.

His kisses gentled, even as his big frame shuddered. Much of his weight rested on his forearms, protecting her. But his lower body held her fast. "We're on even ground then, because I don't know what the hell we're doing. Don't be frightened of me, my brave, bighearted Dani. I won't let anything happen to you, I swear."

She kissed him then. Some might have called it a kiss of surrender. Dani knew it was more. It was taking what she wanted despite the inevitable consequences. "Make love to me, Nathaniel."

Whatever gentleness he had shown her in the beginning burned up in the fire of simple, undeniable, lustful pleasure. He pumped hard, rapidly. Her first climax hit sharp and sudden. She cried out and moaned as he carried her through it. But Nathaniel was far from done. They tumbled to the soft carpet with Dani on top. His fingers dug into her hips with bruising strength.

His chest heaved. His eyes blazed. "Ride me, honey. Find what you need. I can wait...maybe."

She took him at his word. It was exhilarating and frantic and more wildly pleasurable than she had ever imagined. Twice more, she climaxed. With the last one, Nathaniel came as well, dragging her down to his chest and holding her in arms of steel as he groaned and thrust his way to the finish line.

When it was over, the only sound in the room was their labored breathing and the gentle hum of the gas logs.

Dani's bottom, exposed to the air, started to get cold. She dared not move. If she did, she would have to face Nathaniel. How could she do that?

How would she ever again be able to look him in the eye and pretend they were nothing more than boss and assistant?

Thank God she had already been sending out résumés. Perhaps tonight was her subconscious way of making sure she followed through on her decision to leave New Century. Nothing about Nathaniel had changed. He'd warned her as much at the dinner table. Dani would have to be the one to make smart decisions.

But how? How was a woman supposed to resist a man who combed his fingers through her hair and seemed not to notice that she had the beginnings of muffin top? He made love to her like she was a pool of life-giving water, and he'd been lost in the Sahara. She'd felt his desperation. His whole body shook, and not just with orgasm, but as he caressed her breasts and kissed her so sweetly.

Doggedly, she told herself that Nathaniel was right. *None* of this was real. They were playacting. Making the best of a bad situation, or two bad situations, if you counted Peaches. The snow and the child. Blizzards and babies and boners, oh, my.

The irreverent thought made her giggle.

Nathaniel noticed, of course. He opened one eye and glared up at her. "I hope you're not laughing at me. I might point out you're in a very vulnerable position."

She sobered rapidly. "No, sir, boss." Brushing her lips across his stubbly jaw, she played the aggressor. "Merely wondering how long I have to wait for round two."

Disengaging their bodies, he scrambled to his feet and pulled her up with two hands. "I have a great shower. Lots of settings on the showerhead. You'll love it."

"Um..."

He lifted her chin. "Talk to me, little Christmas elf. I'm having the damnedest time reading you right now."

She shrugged, trying to pretend she wasn't naked. "Showers are kind of personal. I'm not exactly a *sharing* kind of person when it comes to personal hygiene."

Nathaniel's lips quirked. "It's a good thing you're cute."

"Why is that?"

He kissed her nose. "Because you're a lot of work."

"I am *not*," she said, affronted. "Have I complained once about being kidnapped and forced to be your nanny?"

"You've been a saint," he said gravely. "But I was talking about your emotional state. I've seen pictures of a sphinx who's less inscrutable than you are. Two days ago we were in the office doing the usual, and now you tell me you've been fantasizing about me. Who knew?" He sounded aggrieved.

It was too perfect an opening not to ask. She stroked one of his biceps, loving the way her caress made him shiver. "I'm curious. Did you ever fantasize about *me* when we were at the office?"

Doors slammed shut in Nathaniel's brain. *Danger, danger.* He drew in a ragged breath. "Hell, yes. But that was very unprofessional on my part." He backed away. "I think you're right about the shower. If you don't mind, I'll go first. If Peaches wakes up in the meantime, I'll give her a bottle so you can get some sleep."

He didn't remember how he got to his bedroom. He must have released Dani. He must have grabbed his shirt and pants, because they were clutched in his hands.

Swallowing back the taste of dread and panic, he showered quickly and changed into jeans and an old college sweatshirt. Despite the hot water, he was cold through to the bone.

The expression in Dani's eyes when she looked up at him hadn't been inscrutable at all. It encompassed vulnerability and shy affection and probably a million questions. Simple questions any woman had the right to ask when she had just surrendered her body to a man she should be able to trust. A man who had vowed to protect her.

For ten minutes, he paced the confines of his bedroom, formulating a game plan, deciding what to say. If he and Dani continued to have sex, she would expect things from him. Things he likely couldn't or wouldn't give. But if he came right out and said he was only playing around, he would leave himself open to her recriminations, maybe even reprisals.

She was a decent woman. With a kind heart. Still, he and she together had crossed a line. A line that made him as vulnerable as his father had been all those years ago.

Dani wouldn't sue him. He wouldn't lose his company. The chances of that happening were infinitesimal.

Without warning, a distant memory flashed, one he had forgotten in the mists of time. A woman in a professional, powder blue suit occupied the witness stand, her face hard and cold as she listed Nathaniel's father's transgressions, demanding vengeance. Nathaniel, almost eighteen by that time, had been sitting in the back row of the courtroom.

His mother was hospitalized. His father was a broken man, forced to appear before judge and jury and have his life's work torn to shreds. Nathaniel hadn't known how to help either of his parents.

A sound from outside the sanctuary of his bedroom jerked him back to the present. He had to go back to the den and face Dani. Squaring his shoulders, he told himself not to overreact. All he had to do was tread carefully. As soon as the snow melted and Ophelia retrieved the baby, life would go back to normal.

When he found his two female houseguests, they were ensconced on the sofa, wrapped in an afghan, Dani was wearing his shirt again. Her eyes were closed, her head resting against the back of the seat. Peaches was awake, noisily downing a bottle of formula. The lights were off. Only the flames from the fire illuminated the room.

Carefully, Nathaniel sat down beside woman and child. He put a hand on Dani's knee. She was sitting cross-legged with the baby in her lap. "You okay?" he asked softly. "Do you want me to take her?"

Dani opened her eyes and stared at him. He bore her scrutiny stoically. His assistant was a smart woman. She had to know something was wrong. Thankfully, she let it slide. "We're fine, Nathaniel. Why don't you go back to bed? You have no idea how long Peaches will be staying with you, and unfortunately, I won't be around to help much longer. You should get sleep while you can."

He inhaled sharply. Apparently they weren't going to discuss his earlier behavior. Instead, Dani let it be known very plainly she was not going to linger in his home waiting for scraps of his attention and affection. There was a quiet dignity about her that shamed him. The open, joyful response he'd seen in her after their intimate encounter was gone.

Moving his hand from her knee, he tried to breathe naturally. The gaping hole in his chest made that difficult. Had he crushed the only person in his life who actually cared about him?

Dani lifted the baby onto her shoulder and patted her back. "How will you go about finding Ophelia?"

"I've contacted a private investigator. Needless to say, he's not eager to leave his family on Christmas. He's promised to get to work on the case first thing Monday. I'm confident Ophelia's still in the city. After all, how far could she get? If we're trapped, so is she."

"Good point." Dani stood, holding the baby carefully. Peaches had nodded off. "I think she'll sleep a few more hours now. We'll see you in the morning."

Nathaniel jumped to his feet. "Wait," he said hoarsely.

Dani turned back, but her posture was defensive, and she held the child as a shield. "What, Nathaniel? What do you want?"

On the surface, it was almost a rhetorical question. As if she knew he didn't know why he had stopped her. But then again, maybe she was demanding more. Explanations. Assurances. Unfortunately, he had none to give.

"It's December 25 already," he said, feeling foolish and desperate. "Merry Christmas, Dani."

Her smile was wistful, perhaps even sad. "Merry Christmas, Nathaniel."

After that, he let her go, because it was the right thing to do. He had no right to coax her into lingering so he would have someone to talk to. He liked being alone. He enjoyed his own company. It was only the snow and the holiday and the baby throwing him off balance.

He prowled the condo, unable to contemplate sleep. If he hadn't been such an ass, Dani might have been in his bed this very moment, her cuddly, warm body pressed against his as they dozed in between bouts of hot, satisfying sex.

What would it take to win a woman like Dani? For one thing, he would have to change virtually everything about himself. Dani would expect open communication and an honest exchange of feelings and emotions. The thought made him shudder. He'd perfected the art of walling himself off from the world. It was too late to change now.

Walking alone was the only way he knew.

Dani cried herself to sleep. When she awoke four hours later, her head ached and she faced the inescapable conviction she was her own worse enemy. She *knew* what the boss was like, perhaps better than anyone else in his life. Why on earth had she asked him such a stupid question? *Did you ever fantasize about me when we were at the office?*

The raw honesty of his answer had revealed the extent of his conflicted emotions. Nathaniel was a man. Men were creatures of the moment. They compartmentalized things in their brains. Work, sex, food, sleep. The only reason she and Nathaniel ended up being intimate was the result of an unlikely set of circumstances.

As she changed a wet diaper and blew raspberries on a soft baby tummy, she fretted. She needed to get out of this condo. The sooner, the better. If she had sex with her boss a second time, she'd never convince herself to leave. Even worse, she might ignore all common sense and be put in the ignominious position of being *asked* to leave.

That wasn't going to happen. Ever. She might not be able to eradicate her feelings for the man down the hall, but he didn't have to know he was breaking her heart into jagged shards that would never properly fit back together.

Moving to the window, she twitched aside the sheers and looked out. The thaw was supposed to begin today, in theory. High of thirty-eight. Peeks of sunshine. So far, the skies were gray. The coating of ice on top of fifteen inches of snow meant the city was still obliterated. Only the most intrepid would venture out on Christmas Day.

When she closed the curtains and turned around, Nathaniel was standing in the doorway of the guest room. He held out a shopping bag with a quizzical smile on his face. "Your new friend, Reggie, the doorman, came through for us. He dropped off all these baby things a few minutes ago. I thanked him."

"And gave him a big fat Christmas tip, I hope."

"Of course."

"Too bad he has to work the holiday."

Nathaniel nodded. "At least he's only here until two. Several of them are dividing shifts today so no one gets stuck the whole time."

"I'm glad." Dani clutched Peaches like a lifeline. She had worried about imagining Nathaniel naked. The reality was much worse. He was fully dressed in khakis and a white button-front shirt with the sleeves rolled up. His tanned arms, lightly dusted with dark hair, were very masculine, as was the high-end gold watch on his left wrist. But that wasn't the bad part. What made her stomach do sickening flips and flops was this new awareness between them. She couldn't explain it, but it was *there*.

While she stood by the bed trying not to blush, Nathaniel upended the shopping bag and dumped a pile of baby clothes on the bed. "Good news, kid," he said with a chuckle. "You finally get to wear something new."

"Now, if only Reggie had access to my size," Dani joked. The fact that she was modeling another of Nathaniel's soft cotton dress shirts over the same gray thermal pants put her at a distinct disadvantage.

Nathaniel shot her a grin, his expression smug.

"It's still early," he said. "I'm sure Santa hasn't forgotten you, Dani."

She had no clue what that meant. But she wasn't in the mood for flirty repartee. Today was going to be Christmas without the feels.

To keep things on an impersonal track, she propped Peaches on her hip and began sorting through the clothing. Like most baby things, the rompers and sleepers and adorable dresses were mostly in mint condition. At this age, infants grew so fast, it was almost impossible to wear an outfit enough times to do any damage.

Nathaniel stood beside her, making her clumsy and nervous. He picked up a tiny green dress with candy canes appliqued at the hem. "I vote for this one," he said. "Perfect for Peaches's first Christmas Day."

Casually, Dani moved aside, putting a few feet between herself and temptation. "I agree. Why don't you do the honors?"

He blanched. "Me? I have big hands. This stuff looks like doll clothes. You'd better do it. If you don't mind."

Dani hesitated. "Well…"

"What's the problem?"

"I'm leaving when the snow melts, Nathaniel," she said bluntly. "You'll have to do all this yourself."

His expression gave new meaning to the term poker face. "I'll worry about that when the time comes. Besides, Peaches would rather have you dress her right now. She's more comfortable with you."

Dani laid the baby on the bed and quickly switched out the sleeper for the green dress. "Oh, my gosh. Look how cute she is. Hold her, Nathaniel. Let me take a picture." She grabbed her smartphone while Nathaniel made silly faces at Peaches and scooped up the little girl who might or might not be his daughter.

The sight of the big, macho man holding the small, smiling baby made her heart squeeze. They looked right together.

Moments later, Dani tucked the phone in her pocket and managed a casual smile. "If you two are okay for the moment, I'll put breakfast in the oven. Did I smell coffee brewing? Please say yes."

"Plenty for both of us," Nathaniel said. He rubbed noses with the baby. "This beauty and I will be in my office taking care of a little business. Come find us when it's ready."

She stared at him. Something in his voice gave her a little fillip of excitement. "Christmas secrets, Nathaniel?"

Seven

Nathaniel smiled, his expression deliberately bland. "Maybe yes, maybe no. I won't be long."

In his office, he spread a blanket on the floor. He'd grabbed it up from the pile on Dani's bed. "Play with your rattle, little one. I've got to wrap a package."

Reggie had proved to be quite accommodating when Nathaniel explained the situation. The overnight delivery had been signed for, and the doorman had sent up Christmas paper and tape. Unfortunately, turning out eye-catching packages was not in Nathaniel's skill set. He'd been a Boy Scout, but tying knots was a long way from handling thick, glossy paper and recalcitrant ribbon.

At last, he was satisfied. He held up the large rectangle and examined it. "What do you think, Peaches? I'm counting on this to win points with a certain prickly woman."

The baby gummed a pink-and-green teether from the drugstore enthusiastically, but didn't endorse Nathaniel's efforts. "I know," he said glumly. "It's probably too little, too late, but she deserves a merry Christmas, even if I *am* a Scrooge."

Since Peaches was in a mood to be cooperative, Nathaniel did a quick check of email, looking over his shoulder guiltily. There was more to life than work. He knew that. Trouble was, up until this particular odd Christmas, work was all he'd ever had on a day like today.

Half an hour later, Dani showed up, flushed and bright-eyed. "Everything's on the table," she said. "Come and eat."

Fortunately, he'd hidden the box behind a tall wooden file cabinet. Even when Dani crouched to pick up the baby, the gift was out of sight. Timing was everything.

In the kitchen, Dani had opted for casual, preparing two places at the granite counter island instead of in the dining room. The room smelled of cinnamon and yeast. "Wow," he said, inhaling with enjoyment. "You went to a lot of trouble." The mimosas were especially tempting, particularly since no one had to go anywhere.

On the other hand, he needed a clear head to negotiate a peace treaty with his beautiful houseguest. He took a stool and held out his hands. "I'll hold her while you eat."

Dani shook her head. "We can both eat. I think she'll be happy in her carrier for a little bit."

Either Dani was a gourmet cook or Nathaniel was starving or both. The streusel-topped coffee cake was warm and fragrant and tasted like heaven on a plate. He was on his third piece before he noticed Dani watching him with a grin.

He stopped dead, his fork halfway to his mouth. "Sorry," he mumbled. "I did leave some for you."

Her sunny smile was the first open, uncomplicated one he'd gotten from her since their encounter in the middle of the night. "It's quite all right. A cook likes to know her efforts are appreciated."

Deliberately finishing the last bite on his plate, he wiped the corner of his mouth with his napkin, drained his glass and reached across the small space separating them to stroke his thumb across her cheek. "I appreciate the hell out of you, my little Christmas elf."

Dani turned bright red and busied herself with the baby. "A simple thank-you will suffice," she muttered.

"What shall we do between now and lunch?" he asked in his most genial Christmas host voice. "When Peaches takes a nap, all sorts of things come to mind." He was treading a line between forcing Dani to remember the good parts of last night and hoping like hell she would overlook the bad ones.

"I really need to talk to my parents," she said, not taking the bait. "To see what the plans are for Tuesday. Perhaps you could entertain the baby while I do that. Afterward, I'll feed her and put her down."

"Of course."

To his disappointment and dismay, Dani handed off the kid and disappeared into her bedroom. Had Nathaniel spooked her, or was the excuse a genuine one?

He couldn't exactly listen at the door. Since he

was too jumpy to sit down for any length of time, he cleared the breakfast dishes with one hand and loaded the dishwasher. Fortunately, there was no one around to reprimand him when he sneaked a few more bites of cake.

By the time Dani finally reappeared forty-five minutes later, the baby was getting fussy. Instead of handing her over, Nathaniel decided it was time for him to step up his game. "Let's go to the den," he said. "We don't want to waste that world-class tree. I'll feed the baby, and you can pick a movie. How's that?"

Dani seemed dubious, but she followed his lead. Nathaniel didn't bother with the sofa. He picked the recliner and got comfortable with Peaches in his lap. The baby, as always, guzzled her bottle and conked out.

Dani flipped through his Blu-ray collection and finally settled on one of the original Star Wars movies. He didn't have a single one of the romantic comedies that most women liked, so it was a good thing his guest seemed to share his taste in classic sci-fi/fantasy.

The opening credits had barely finished rolling before the second female in the room fell asleep.

Nathaniel grinned wryly. So much for being a stimulating companion. He rubbed the baby's head. "Were you awake a lot during the night, little scamp? Or is Dani tired for another reason?"

His body tightened and his breath caught as lust roared in uninvited. His den was a far different place in the middle of the day than in the dark of night, but it was difficult not to remember holding a naked Dani in his arms and making love to her like a madman.

Hell. Why hadn't he stayed in the kitchen where the atmosphere was far less charged?

He watched the movie, but he'd seen it half a dozen times. It was far more satisfying to study the woman sleeping a few feet away. To a stranger, this scene would have seemed perfectly normal. Only Nathaniel and Dani knew how very abnormal it was.

She had made no bones about her plans to leave him. If memory served, Dani was using vacation days this week to spend time with her family. They certainly wouldn't understand if, at the last minute, New Century Tech demanded her attention.

No, work wasn't the answer. If he were going to

keep Dani here, he'd have to try something risky. Maybe tell the truth. He didn't want to be alone this week. Not after he'd had a taste of what the holidays *could* be like.

In the meantime, he'd be content with the status quo.

Dani slept for half an hour and woke with a start. Her cheek was creased from the trim on the sofa arm, and her hair was mussed. "Sorry," she said, adorably flustered. "What did I miss?"

He laughed softly, careful not to wake Peaches. "Nothing you haven't seen before." He picked up the remote and hit Pause. He and Dani had known each other forever. They didn't need a movie for distraction, did they?

"Do you want me to take her?" Dani asked. "I've had a nap. It's your turn."

"I'm fine. Don't worry about me."

"If you say so."

An awkward silence fell. Maybe he was wrong about the movie.

He debated his options. The next move could make things better or worse. It surprised him that he couldn't predict the outcome. In a business negotiation, he would have known. But not now.

"Dani?"

"Hmm?" She stared at the fireplace, her expression pensive.

"Do you mind grabbing something from my office? I don't want to move and wake her."

"Of course." She hopped to her feet. "What am I looking for?"

"A large box on the far side of the wooden file cabinet."

"Got it. Back in a flash."

When she returned, she was carrying the package he had tried so hard to wrap artistically. The result looked even more amateurish now. "Thanks," he said.

"What did you do, Nathaniel? Buy her a four-foot teddy bear? This is heavy."

He shrugged. "It's for you. Merry Christmas, Dani."

She froze, her gaze panicked. "Oh, no. I have nothing for you. This is entirely inappropriate. I appreciate the gesture, but I can't accept."

"You don't even know what it is," he said, his tone mild. He knew if he pushed too hard, she might grow even more stubborn in her refusal.

Her hand smoothed the bright red paper, almost a caress. "It doesn't matter what it is," she said. "You gave me a Christmas bonus at the party Friday."

"It's not a present from your boss," he said, losing patience. "Open the box."

"So it's not from you?"

Was she deliberately misunderstanding him, or were they fighting some war he wasn't prepared to engage in? "Yes," he said, jaw clenched. "It *is* from me. To you. Man to woman. Not boss to assistant."

Dani set the box on the floor and curled her legs beneath her. "Did you get whatever this is before we had sex last night?"

"Well, of course, I did," he said unable to hide his irritation. "We've both been a little busy since then."

She studied his face, her expression earnest. What did she want from him?

"I don't think I can accept a present from you, Nathaniel." Her tone was apologetic. "It's a lovely thought, but under these circumstances, I think it would muddy the waters."

He counted to ten and then to fifteen. "Dani..."

"Yes?"

Why did she have to look at him like he was an ogre? What did she think he was going to do to her? Lock her up in a harem?

"Open the damned box. Or you're fired."

"Fat chance," she muttered. "No one else would put up with you."

Apparently losing his temper had convinced her. Strange woman.

She picked at the paper like a Depression-era housewife planning to reuse every scrap of paper and tape and ribbon. The whole process was so slow, he wanted to bellow at her to hurry. It took a great deal of self-control to keep his mouth shut and let her finish.

When she finally removed the box lid and lifted the tissue, her mouth opened in a cute little O of surprise. "Nathaniel. What is all of this?"

Dani didn't know what she had expected. Truthfully, she had handled the gift with all the finesse of a bomb squad technician defusing a dangerous device. She didn't want gifts from Nathaniel. Not when their current situation was so remarkably out of control.

Once she had folded back the tissue, she simply stared at the contents, lifting one thing and the next in amazement. Nothing in the box raised any red flags. If anything, the individual items were extremely practical and thoughtful.

Nathaniel watched her, eagle-eyed, making her uneasy. "Well," he said gruffly. "What do you think? It's not the most exciting present in the world, but you strike me as a very practical woman. Who knows if you'll be able to get back to your apartment before you go to see your family. I tried to think of everything."

Everything was not an exaggeration. Inside the large, deep gift box was a collection of the most elegant clothing and toiletries Dani had ever owned. Dressy black pants in warm wool crepe. A red cashmere V-necked sweater. Two bras and several matching panties, more on the practical than sexy side, but very expensive.

Beneath that were designer jeans, casual tops, elegant sets of flats in black and taupe. Tennis shoes. Socks. A whisper-soft nightgown and matching robe in the palest ivory.

And then the cosmetics, glory be. Cleanser and lotion and mascara and everything else a woman might need to dress herself up for the holidays.

"How on earth did you manage this, Nathaniel?" She stared at him in amazement. "I know you work magic in the business world but this is incredible, even for you."

He shrugged, but she could tell her reaction pleased him. "I have a business associate whose wife works at Neiman Marcus. I called her first thing yesterday morning and told her what had happened with the blizzard and being stranded. I explained in general terms what I wanted to give you. She made it all happen."

"In the snow."

"Yep. I was very persuasive."

"This must have cost a fortune." She frowned slightly. "The snow was going to melt eventually. You know this wasn't necessary."

"It *was* necessary," he said forcefully. "Your holiday plans were wrecked. You've had to help care for a baby who is not yours. You've worked out grocery lists and prepared wonderful meals. This was the least I could do."

Dani set the heavy box aside and went to crouch beside his chair. "Thank you, Nathaniel," she whispered, her throat tight with emotion. Clearly he had gone to a great deal of trouble. The sizes were all correct, too. "For a man who bears a remarkable resemblance to Scrooge, you've done a lovely job with this Christmas surprise." She kissed him softly on the cheek. "I don't know what to say. I'm touched."

He grumbled beneath his breath. "Babies sure as hell cramp a guy's style."

She grinned. "You were hoping my gratitude would translate to sex?"

"Nothing quite so crude." He winced. "But I did hope you wouldn't be mad at me anymore. I want you to be happy, Dani."

She noted that he didn't add the words *with me*. Maybe she was being too picky. "I am happy," she said quietly, brushing a lock of his hair from his forehead. He was holding the baby and couldn't respond physically, but his gaze seared her with its intensity. "Do you mind if I go take a shower and try on some of these things? I can't wait. Not that I don't appreciate the loan of your wardrobe," she said hastily.

He chuckled softly, caressing her visually, giving her goose bumps. "You look fine to me just like you are, but sure. Knock yourself out."

Dani practically danced down the hall. After

two whole days of feeling grubby and unsophis-
ticated, she was finally going to be able to meet
Nathaniel on level ground. After a super quick
shower during which she kept her hair dry, she
put on the new undies and tried the red sweater
and black pants. Everything fit perfectly.

Instead of twisting her hair up in a messy knot,
she took the time to brush it over and over again
until it swung thick and shiny at her shoulders.
Too much makeup seemed like overkill at this
point, but she used the mascara, and she added
berry-red lip gloss to match her sweater. In the
mirror, her reflection wasn't half-bad.

When she returned to the den, Peaches was
awake and playing happily with a teething ring.
Nathaniel's eyes widened when he saw Dani.
"You look stunning," he said quietly. "Red is a
great color on you."

"Nothing like new clothes to give a woman a
boost. Thanks again."

"It was the least I could do."

"Are you getting hungry?"

"I could eat."

The stilted conversation was at odds with the
almost palpable hunger coursing between them.

Dani trembled. "I'll put Christmas dinner to-gether. It will end up being a midafternoon meal, but we can snack later if we get hungry. Do you mind if I open a bottle of wine?"

"Mi casa es su casa," Nathaniel said. "What-ever you want." His words were warm, caressing.

In the kitchen, Dani was torn. Last night she had made use of the dining room for their din-ner, and Nathaniel had freaked out. It didn't seem right, though, to have Christmas lunch at the kitchen counter. So no matter how skittish her boss was, she went right ahead with her holiday preparations the same way she would have if this were an ordinary situation.

She whisked together brown gravy. When it was warm and bubbling, she sliced the leftover roast beef in small pieces and added the meat to the pot. Peeling potatoes gave her too much time to think. Tonight the baby would fall asleep, and Dani would find herself alone with Nathaniel again. What was she going to do if he wanted sex? Could she hold him off? Did she want to say no?

Maybe she wanted to enjoy whatever time they

had left in this odd and emotionally charged situation.

In less than an hour, she managed to put together a respectable meal—nothing too fancy, but far better than the peanut butter they had dined on the first night. Open-faced roast beef sandwiches on sourdough toast. Fluffy mashed potatoes. Cranberry salad and, of course, plenty of leftover pecan pie for dessert.

The end result was gratifying.

Nathaniel and Peaches appeared just as she was putting the finishing touches on the dinner table. Her boss frowned.

"What now?" Dani sighed. "I left the tree in the den. Nothing holidayish, I swear."

"It's not that," he said. "I just realized I'm going to owe you half a dozen fancy dinners at four-star restaurants to repay you for all you've done."

"Sit down and don't be ridiculous," she said. "I like eating as much as the next person. If I'd been at my parents' house, I would have worked even harder. My mom puts on quite a spread."

Nathaniel consumed most of his meal without speaking. It was impossible to read his mood. Once again, Dani was glad to have the baby as a diversion. Breaking bread together was actually a very intimate thing to do. This time, Nathaniel was the one holding the child and eating one-handed.

At last, Dani couldn't bear the silence any longer. "What are your plans for tomorrow?" she asked. "Assuming the weather does what they say it will."

He stood abruptly. "I'm going to grab some pie. You want yours now or later?"

"Later," she said. Was he in that much of a hurry for dessert, or did he not want to answer her question?

When Nathaniel returned, he held Peaches in one arm and a generous serving of gooey pie in the other hand.

Dani raised an eyebrow. "You'll make yourself sick," she warned.

His smile was wicked. "What a way to go."

While she appreciated the fact that her boss enjoyed her cooking, bigger issues loomed on the horizon. Sex. The baby. Dani's imminent departure.

"I talked to my mom on speakerphone while I was cooking," she said.

Nathaniel swallowed a bite of pie. "Oh?"

"They thought about postponing our family Christmas until Wednesday, but my siblings can't be off work that day. So we're definitely celebrating Tuesday. I've promised to be there by ten in the morning."

"Sounds good."

Such a bullheaded, frustrating man. "Look at me, Nathaniel."

He lifted his head and eyed her with a deceptively mild expression. "What's wrong?"

"Nothing. Not exactly. But I'm worried about leaving you alone with the baby. Single parenting is hard for anybody."

"Especially a clueless male like me?"

"I didn't say that. Peaches is getting very comfortable with you and vice versa." She shook her head, wondering why she was obsessing about this. Peaches wasn't her problem. Still, it knotted her stomach to think about leaving man and baby to fend for themselves. "The trip from here to home is an hour and a half, give or take. Normally, I would simply drive up Tuesday morning. But first of all, we don't know how much snow and ice will melt tomorrow, and second of all, any standing water will probably refreeze tomorrow night."

"I'd say you're right."

"So I'll have to go tomorrow afternoon."

"Whatever you need to do."

"Do you even care that I'm leaving?" she cried.

He stood up abruptly, nearly knocking over his chair. Her statement echoed in the small dining room.

"This was never supposed to happen." He waved a hand. "I get it. You want to be with your family. I won't stand in your way. You have no obligation whatsoever to me or even to Peaches."

He was saying all the right words, but he was breaking her heart. He was so very much alone. Dani took a deep breath and gambled. "Come with me to visit my parents," she begged. "You and Peaches. I can't bear the thought of leaving you here alone."

Eight

Nathaniel blinked, feeling his anger and frustration winnow away to be replaced by something even more unsettling. He knew what it was like to have someone feel sorry for him, but it had been a very long time since he had been on the receiving end of that reaction. He didn't much care for it. There were any number of things he wanted from Dani. Pity wasn't one of them.

"I have to be at work on Tuesday," he said calmly, careful to reveal nothing of the confusion tearing him apart. "New Century Tech will be open for business. I have employees."

"What about the baby?"

Dani's dogged insistence on planning was commendable, but since he didn't have any of the answers she wanted, his only recourse was stonewalling. "I'll work something out. Besides, the baby will only be with me a day or two longer. I'm confident the investigator will find Ophelia quickly."

"I'm all in favor of positive thinking," Dani said wryly, "but that's not much of a strategy. Seriously, Nathaniel, come to Gainesville with me. It won't be odd if you show up. Mom and Dad often have stray guests at the dinner table, even at the holidays. We wouldn't sleep overnight at the house, of course. There are several nice hotels nearby."

"I appreciate what you're trying to do," he said, "but I'll be fine."

The combative subject was dropped by unspoken consent when Peaches decided she was hungry. Dani fed the baby while Nathaniel cleaned up the kitchen. Already, they had blown through most of the groceries he'd brought home on Saturday. Even the baby supplies were getting low.

When the kitchen was clean and the baby

asleep on his bedroom floor, he realized he had to get out of the condo or risk making love to Dani. If they had sex again, she would make assumptions about the two of them. He wasn't ready for that.

The wonderful meal he had consumed sat like lead in his stomach. "I'm going to the store for round two," he said suddenly. "Make a list. I'll be back in a minute."

"Oh, but—"

He exited the warm, cozy kitchen before Dani could say anything else. When he had donned his parka and ski pants and gloves, he went back for the list. "Is it ready?" he asked, not looking at her. The cherry-red sweater he'd given her for Christmas clung to all the right places. Looking at her breasts was a bad idea.

"You can't go to the store, Nathaniel."

"Of course, I can."

"It's Christmas Day. I'm sure there might be some places open here and there, but probably not in walking distance. Quit worrying. I can stretch the food we have left until Monday afternoon. We can always do something simple tomorrow like bacon and eggs and pancakes."

He stripped off his outerwear a piece at a time, feeling ridiculous. "I keep forgetting it's Christmas," he muttered.

Dani shook her head in amusement. "First I've inundated you with too much Christmas, and now you say you forgot about it entirely. Make up your mind."

He shot her a glance, feeling his resolve wane. "I needed to get out of the house," he said bluntly. "Away from you. It wasn't really about the groceries."

"Oh." She looked stricken.

"I want you, Dani. Under the circumstances, it doesn't seem fair to you."

"Because?"

"Because you can't say no without causing tension between us." When she didn't say a word, he lifted his shoulders and rotated his neck. "Never mind. I'm going for a walk. Call me if there's an emergency."

Desperate to get away, he turned on his heel and strode out of the room. He made it to the front door before Dani intervened. The relief he experienced when he heard her voice call to him was overwhelming and inexplicable.

"Don't go out in the cold, Nathaniel. Stay with me."

He turned around slowly. She smiled faintly, but her eyes held secrets. Clearing his throat, he tossed his gloves on the console by the door and ran his hands through his hair. "If I stay, I'll make love to you. Sooner or later. You know that's true."

She swallowed visibly. "Yes."

"Things between us are complicated. You have to be sure."

Waiting for her answer was the longest five seconds of his life.

"I can't think of a better way to spend Christmas," she whispered.

The look on her face made him damned glad she had stopped him. "Now?" he asked hoarsely.

"Shouldn't we wait until tonight?" she said, her wide-eyed expression betrayed the struggle between madness and common sense.

"Maybe. But I can't." Deliberately, he began undressing, not only his cold-weather gear, but his socks and shoes and belt and everything down to his shirt and pants. Dani watched him intently, her cheeks flushed.

The door to his bedroom was open down the hall. They would hear the baby if she woke. "Say something," he demanded. "Tell me what you want."

"I'm not sure *what* I want," she said, wincing. He heard the truth in her words. "Maybe I just need you to know that *I* know."

His hands stilled on his shirt buttons. "Know what?"

"That we're taking a moment out of time. Period. That this ends when we walk out your front door tomorrow. I get it. You don't have to worry about me, Nathaniel. You're a sexy, interesting man. I want to be with you. But I won't make any uncomfortable demands. No awkward endings. You have my word."

Her ability to see right through to the deepest layers of his psyche alarmed him. The trouble was, he didn't have any pretty speeches to say in reply. Dani was one hundred percent correct. They had today and tonight and maybe tomorrow.

After that, the snow melted, the baby was reunited with her mother and Nathaniel went back to being top dog at New Century Tech. Business as usual.

He held out a hand. "Come here, little elf."

The choice on his part to remain still was deliberate. He needed Dani's physical assurance that she wanted to take this step.

Instead of taking his hand, she flung herself at him, wrapped her arms around his neck and knocked the breath from his lungs. "Merry Christmas, Nathaniel."

He hugged her instinctively. Finding her mouth with his, he dove in for the taste that was his new addiction. "God, you're sweet."

She bit his neck, sharply enough to bruise. "I'm not particularly interested in *sweet* right now. Take me, Nathaniel. Show me the real you. I won't break, and I won't run away."

"God help us both," he muttered. He kissed her wildly, sliding his hands beneath her sweater and finding warm, soft breasts. "You didn't have to wear a bra," he complained.

"Your fault." Her voice was muffled against his collarbone. "New clothes. Didn't want to hurt your feelings."

Clumsily, he tugged the sweater over her head

and unfastened the offending undergarment. When Dani was bare from the waist up, he put his hands on her hips and dragged her against him. "I'm too close to the edge," he groaned. "Embarrassingly so. Give me a minute."

Dani shook her head and leaned back to look up at him, her eyes bright with pleasure. "I like driving you mad," she said. "It gives me power."

She was joking. He knew that. He *knew* Dani. Still, the words sent a frisson of unease down his spine. Shaking off the sense of foreboding, he kissed her gently. "Take all the power you want, little elf. Tonight, you're mine."

Dani was under no illusions. She could only take what Nathaniel gave freely. There was a part of him that was off-limits to her, to everyone. She would have to be satisfied with the very appealing bits and pieces he offered. If the next twenty-four hours were to be their swan song, this unlikely pairing would be as special as she could make it.

Stuffing her doubts into a dark closet, she cupped his face in her hands. "You know how in movies the hero sometimes takes the heroine up against the front door, because he can't make it any farther before he has sex with her?"

Nathaniel rolled his eyes, but he grinned. "I get the general idea."

"Well…" She removed his shirt and pressed her naked breasts to his wonderfully hard, warm chest. "I was thinking we might try that."

He shuddered when she linked her arms around his waist and slid her fingertips inside his jeans, caressing his lower back. "I *could* use some exercise," he said soberly.

"Sex burns calories," she muttered. Perhaps they might just stand here like this all afternoon. She felt safe and warm, as if nothing bad would ever happen.

Nathaniel took her idea and ran with it. Before she blinked twice, he had her pants and undies down her legs. "Step out of them," he demanded.

There must have been a draft in the foyer. Gooseflesh broke out all over her body, and her nipples went on high alert. Stark naked, she wrapped her arms around her breasts. "Stop," she said hastily. "Your pants have to go, too."

He lifted an eyebrow, kneeling at her feet. "I've seen one or two of those movies. The guy keeps his pants on sometimes. You know...'cause he's in such a hurry."

She chuckled, despite her tendency to hyperventilate. "Now you're mocking me."

"A little bit." He stood and shucked his trousers and boxers casually, removing a couple of condoms from his pocket along the way. "If my back goes out from these shenanigans, you'll have to carry me to bed."

The humor didn't really compute. A naked Nathaniel Winston was even more powerful and intimidating than the one in the tailored suits and pristine white dress shirts. He was a male animal in his prime.

If she hadn't been breathless with longing and terrified the baby was going to wake up at the most inopportune moment, Dani might have taken the time to study her lover's body in detail. As it was, urgency overtook any desire to savor the moment.

"How do we do this?" she asked, the words embarrassingly weak and shaky.

Nathaniel's smile took all the starch out of her knees. "You let me worry about the logistics, honey. Right now I'm going to kiss you until you forget your name." With a nonchalance Dani could never have managed in a million years, he took care of the condom and tossed aside the packet.

Dani sighed when he folded her in his arms and held her loosely, brushing her forehead with a tender kiss.

"My lips are down here," she pointed out, trying to speed things along.

"I never noticed how bossy you are."

"I never noticed how slow you are."

Without warning, he scooped her up and palmed her bottom. She buried her face in the crook of his neck and wrapped her legs around his waist. His thick erection pressed against her. He shuddered and panted, his entire body rigid. "More foreplay later, I swear."

"I believe you."

The muscles in his arms corded and bunched as he lifted her slowly and carefully lowered her onto his sex. The feeling was indescribable. Despite their pretense that Dani was calling the shots, this particular position put Nathaniel irrevocably in charge.

Gravity worked in his favor. The fit was tight,

almost uncomfortable. Dani started to shake as nerves and arousal duked it out in her stomach.

Nathaniel cursed and groaned. "Too much?" he asked, jaw clenched, the words barely audible.

"No, no, no…but don't forget the door."

He staggered and laughed and stumbled forward until Dani's bottom made contact with cold, hard wood. "You asked for this, elf." With purchase now to aid his mission, Nathaniel thrust forcefully.

Dani held on, fingernails scoring his shoulders. Eyes closed, lungs starved for oxygen, she let him take her savagely, recklessly. It was too much in one second and not enough the next. Laughing, sobbing, she clung to him until she felt her orgasm rise up from the depths of her soul. It flashed and burst and consumed her.

A heartbeat later, Nathaniel pummeled his way to his own reward. "God, Dani. Hold on…" His words faded as he shuddered for what seemed like an eternity and finally slumped against her, pinning her to the door that had been the vehicle for her fantasy.

Afterward, she was never sure how long they stood there. Or rather, Nathaniel stood. Dani was limp and exhausted and completely at his mercy. She wouldn't have changed a thing.

In the aftermath of insanity, one thing was clear. She was in love with her boss. If she weren't mistaken, she had been for a very long time.

The blinders came off painfully. For months, she'd been telling herself she had to find new employment. Now she knew why. This was more than a simple crush. She was deeply, irrevocably in lust and love with this virile, complicated man.

She started to tremble and couldn't stop.

Nathaniel read her response as being cold. Without speaking or changing their positions, he carried her down the hall to his bedroom. They scooted past the baby and into the opulent master bathroom. Carefully, he lifted her and set her on her feet. "Was that everything you wanted it to be?"

His teasing smile—along with the smug satisfaction he radiated—made her blush.

"It was lovely," she said primly. "I'll check that off my bucket list."

He kissed her nose. "Something tells me I'd like to see your list if those are the kind of things on it."

"Private," she said airily. "Need-to-know basis, only." *And you don't need to know, Nathaniel Winston, because you won't be around to help me check them off.*

Refusing to ruin their romantic moment with her grief, she twisted her hair into a towel and turned on the water in the shower. "I don't want to get my hair wet. Peaches will be awake soon. Why don't I go first?"

Nathaniel shook his head, his expression brooking no argument. "I'll keep your hair dry, Dani, but you're not getting in *my* shower without me."

"Okay. It's your call." But the shower took a turn she hadn't expected. By the time she reached for the faucet and adjusted the water temperature, her boss-now-lover was hard again, impressively so.

Pretending not to notice, she backed into a corner of the marble enclosure. Grabbing a washcloth, she soaped it and prepared to execute the quickest cleanup on record.

Nathaniel took matters—and the washcloth—out of her hands. "Don't be shy, Dani. Maybe this one is on *my* bucket list."

It was depressing to think he had probably enjoyed shower sex with any number of strange women. But when he gently washed her breasts and then moved lower, her eyes closed and her body went lax with pleasure. After he completed his mission, fore and aft, he used the detachable shower sprayer to rinse her completely. As he had promised, the towel protecting her hair stayed perfectly dry.

"Thank you," she muttered. She felt as if her entire body was covered in one big blush. She'd had sex with the man twice already. Yet still, his touch in this new context left her feeling vulnerable and uncertain.

"Will you do the honors?" He held out the washcloth with a challenging gleam in his eye. Not for the world would Dani let him see how very far out of her depth she was. Ocean deep. Wishing for a life raft. In imminent danger of drowning.

Nathaniel had been careful to point the showerhead away from her. Which meant that she could kneel at his feet and soap him up to her heart's content.

It was a dangerous game they played. Nathaniel clenched his fists, his eyes closed. His head fell back to rest against the wall. The length of him was fascinating—alive, powerful and so very sensitive to her touch.

For a man to allow a woman this level of intimate attention required a level of trust. In one brief moment, Nathaniel had chosen to yield his power for the sweet pleasure a lover's caress could bring. Dani held him in two hands, marveling at a creation that was at once so commonplace and yet so incredibly beautiful and life-giving.

The physical relationship between them was new and short-lived. Cleansing him was one thing. Other more intimate attentions were beyond her comfort level. She brushed a soft kiss across the head of his erection and rose to her feet. "Turn around, so I can finish."

His back was almost as compelling as other parts. Sleek muscles, male sinew and bone, all of it fascinated her. At last, she took the sprayer and removed every soapy bubble. "All done," she croaked.

Nathaniel spun around so quickly she gasped. He dragged her against him and kissed her hard, desperately. She felt the tang of blood in her mouth. "Dani," he groaned. "Dani, my sweet Dani." Maneuvering her like a rag doll, he turned her to the wall and placed her hands above her head, palms flat on the slick, wet surface. "Don't move."

One breathless heartbeat later she felt him enter her from behind. This time the theme was slow possession, so measured and deliberate she wanted to claw the wall. Her climax built in gentle swells and waves, one after the next. Nathaniel drew back and pushed in again, his size and force stimulating sensitive flesh already tender from their earlier lovemaking.

His big hands gripped her hips. "I won't let you forget this," he growled. "I'll take you again and again today until you beg me for more, and then we'll start all over again."

The provocative mental picture he painted sent her over the edge. She cried out and tried to stay still, but the end was too much for both of them, the shower floor too slick. Nathaniel scooped her up, took two steps out and deposited her on the thick, fluffy bathroom rug. He moved between her thighs with frantic haste. "Now," he moaned. "Come again, come with me."

* * *

Nathaniel slumped on top of Dani and tried to remember how to breathe. In the other room, the baby stirred. Damn it. How did couples with babies ever talk? No that he wanted to talk, not really. He was screwed and he knew it.

Dani would have to go to another division, another boss. The idea made his skin crawl. But he wasn't in denial. There was no way he could work with her now and not be constantly sidelined by lust. Already, he wanted her day and night.

The depth of that wanting scared him more than anything he had ever faced. No woman had ever mattered to him this way. He'd never allowed it. Now, though, he was torn between wanting to keep Dani at arm's length and being wildly jealous of any other man at NCT who might cross her path.

Incredulous that he had allowed himself to stray so far from his life's plan, he felt a lick of despair and panic.

He needed to think. He needed a plan. Unfortunately, this entire situation was spiraling madly out of control.

Dani shoved at his shoulders. "Let me go get her, please. She slept forever. I'm sure she's starving."

Rolling to one side, he slung an arm over his eyes and tried not to freak out. In his peripheral vision, he saw Dani take his terry robe from the back of the door and belt it twice around herself. The way her narrow waist flared into a curvy ass was an image he would never get out of his brain. His hands tingled with the need to touch her again.

He decided to let Dani tend to the kid for a few moments while he pulled himself together. Once he was dressed again, he felt marginally more normal. Unfortunately, he couldn't stay in the bathroom forever.

When he opened the door to the bedroom, woman and baby were gone. Made sense. The formula and bottles were in the kitchen. He found his missing houseguests there. Dani perched on a stool. Peaches was in her lap.

Dani didn't look at him, but she muttered a greeting. Her gaze was fixed on the baby. "I've seen how you look at her," she said. "You're already halfway in love with this baby. It's going to hurt like hell if she's not yours, isn't it?"

He poured himself a cup of coffee. "Sharing custody of a child with Ophelia would be a nightmare, so no."

"I wasn't talking about Ophelia. I was talking about you and Peaches. I've watched you with her. Deep down, you wouldn't be too upset if this baby carries your DNA."

"Quit trying to psychoanalyze me, Dani. I'm not a kid person. Never have been. Never will be. The baby is cute. I'll give you that. But believe me, I'll be happy to hand her back to her real parent. Hopefully sooner than later."

The inquisition should have bothered him far more than it did. But his body was relaxed and sated from really great sex, so it was almost impossible to get mad at Dani for weaving her naive theories.

"I do have a Christmas present for you after all," she said. Peaches finished the bottle. Dani put the baby on her shoulder and patted her back. "It's on my phone. Take a look."

The photograph Dani had captured at some point this weekend when he wasn't aware was beautiful. Even he had to admit that. He'd been in the den with the baby showing her the Christmas tree. The damned shot could have made the cover of a parenting magazine. *Man in Love with His New Child. Father Shares the Joys of Christmas with the Next Generation. Innocence and Trust. Daddy and Daughter.*

He clicked out of the photo app and laid the phone on the counter. "Thank you. Text it to me. It will be a good reminder to vet my future bed partners more carefully."

When Dani's face went blank, he cursed. "I'm sorry," he said stiffly. "That was a stupid thing to say. I'm sorry, Dani." He went to her and put his arms around her and the baby. "I'm not usually so clumsy. I was trying to be funny, but it wasn't funny at all. You're the only woman I want in my bed, I swear."

"For now. Not forever."

"I thought we both agreed this was a for-now kind of thing." Was she trying to make him feel guilty? It was working.

"We did. Of course." Dani wriggled free of his embrace and stood. "I think this would be a good time to finish that movie we started earlier."

Nathaniel released her reluctantly. Somehow they had segued from mind-blowing sex in his bedroom to acting like stilted strangers. He knew it was his fault. What he didn't know was how to fix it.

The remainder of Christmas Day passed slowly. Their snowed-in weekend was drawing to a close. Outside, a few of the main thoroughfares had been plowed and salted. Traffic was moving again, albeit slowly. The temperature had climbed above freezing for a few hours, but there was still plenty of snow cover. The side streets would be a mess.

Peaches was content to play on a blanket for long periods of time. She had napped a great deal of the day, so now she was awake and in a good mood.

Nathaniel was glad to have the child as a chaperone. Again and again, he revisited the invitation to accompany Dani to her parents' home. Was there a trap hidden in there, a trap he didn't see?

Dani was the least manipulative woman he knew. Then again, he had allowed her unprecedented access to his private life. Something had changed. Something more than the initiation of a physical relationship. He found himself wanting to lock the door and never let her leave. Here in his condo, he could control the outcome.

Once the real world intruded again, all bets were off.

Christmas supper was leftovers, but damned good leftovers. Afterward, Nathaniel entertained the baby while Dani spoke on the phone again to each of her siblings and her parents. It was clear to him that the Meadows clan was a tight-knit bunch. If Dani showed up with her boss and a baby in tow, wouldn't everyone think it was odd?

Again, he tried to sniff out danger. Finally, he asked Dani outright, "Won't your family think it strange if Peaches and I tag along with you?"

In her red sweater and black pants, Dani looked elegant and not nearly as approachable as the woman wearing his shirts. "Why? Are you thinking about changing your mind?"

"That's not an answer," he pointed out wryly.

Dani wrinkled her nose. "I'm the youngest. My parents have seen it all. Before my sister got married, she dated an insurance salesman with three boys under the age of seven. The man was looking for a built-in babysitter. Fortunately, Angie wised up before it was too late. He wasn't the only weirdo, though. There was a musician in an alternative rock band and a tax accountant turned street preacher."

"Wow."

"Yeah. Angie went through a rebellious stage before she settled down with my brother-in-law, who, by the way, is pretty much a saint."

Nathaniel grinned. "What about your brother?"

"He's not married yet. For the last couple of years, he's been dating a string of short-term partners. Nice women, but they haven't a clue what to do with Jared. He has an IQ in the hundred fifties. The man needs intellectual stimulation, even if he doesn't know it yet."

"I'm sure it will dawn on him eventually."

"We can only hope."

"I'm not sure where I fit in," Nathaniel drawled. "I'm not a musician or much of a churchgoer. But I do temporarily have a baby to look after."

"I've been thinking about that," Dani said earnestly. "If you decide to come with me to Gainesville tomorrow, I'll simply introduce you as my boss. They know your name, of course, because I've spoken about you. I'll say you're caring for a friend's baby and that we got snowed in together. That's all they need to know."

"In their shoes, I might have a lot of questions."

"Even if that were true, they wouldn't make you uncomfortable. My parents are the consummate Southern hosts. They may feed you too much, and you might have to listen to my father's dumb jokes, but no one will put you on the spot."

"I'll think about it," he said.

Dani's pleased expression was its own reward.

At bedtime, they faced an awkward moment. Dani held Peaches, prepared to disappear into her room for the night. Nathaniel stopped her with a hand on her arm. He kissed her cheek. "Sleep in my bed tonight," he muttered.

"Are you sure?" Dani looked up at him searchingly as if she saw every one of his doubts.

"I'm sure."

Nine

An hour and a half later, he wasn't sure at all. Peaches was asleep in her little walled-off nest in the corner. Dani had chosen to get ready for bed in her own room and returned wearing the simple ivory silk gown and robe. She looked young and innocent and disturbingly bridal.

"I know I gave you those," he said gruffly. "But I'd rather have you naked."

Dani lifted an eyebrow. "Maybe if you dim the lights first?" she said, laughing.

"No. I don't think I will." He was counting on the fact that his feisty assistant never backed down from a challenge.

She shot him a glare promising retribution but seconds later stripped down to her bare skin, tossed the night clothes on the nearest chair and scuttled under the covers. "I'm cold," she complained.

The obvious ploy to reverse his command had no effect whatsoever. "I'll warm you up," he said.

Dani had the blanket pulled up to her chin. Her sultry smile promised all sorts of naughty delights.

With shaking hands, he unbuttoned his shirt and unfastened his pants. Having Dani watch him with rapt fascination did good things for a man's ego. When he was completely naked, he let her look her fill. His sex was rigid with anticipation, his body primed and hungry.

"Invite me to come to bed, little elf."

"It's your bed," she pointed out with inescapable logic. "I'm only visiting."

"You look good in there."

It was true. It had been a very long time since *any* woman had graced his condo with her presence. Now he had two females under his roof. No wonder he felt off balance.

Dani's dark, honey hair tumbled across the pillow. Her eyes were heavy-lidded with arousal. She couldn't hide from him. Not anymore.

"When I asked you to sleep with me tonight, I meant that literally," he confessed.

"I know." Her smile was equal parts wistful and wry. "But between the baby waking up at all hours and you waving *that* thing around, I can't imagine either of us will get much rest."

"It's called a penis," he chuckled, climbing underneath the covers and dragging her into his arms. She felt amazing tucked up against him. Feminine curves and soft, soft skin. "This was a very good idea."

"And you're so modest, too."

"Brat."

"Autocrat."

"Shrew."

She laughed softly, curling one arm around his neck and kissing his chin. "I like fighting with you."

"Is that what we're doing?" He rubbed his hands over her rounded butt, squeezing experimentally. "I thought we were negotiating."

She pulled back and stared at him, her expression wry. The lamp on the bedside table was still on, though the bulb was small and the light it cast not bright at all. "Everything I have is yours tonight, Nathaniel," she said softly. "No negotiating necessary. I'm here because I want to be."

Big blue eyes seemed to reflect the knowledge that he was incapable of giving her what she needed. He couldn't let this go too far. Not without risking his heart and his professional life. What did Dani expect from him?

His throat was so tight he had to swallow before he could speak. "I'm glad," he said gruffly.

Giving in to the greatest temptation he had ever known, he let himself wallow in her goodness, her welcome, her much-needed warmth. He had stocked the nearest drawer with a dozen condoms, and even that might not be enough. They came together in every way imaginable, hard and fast, lazy and slow. They dozed from time to time, and then he took her again.

He didn't know what love was. Surely not this desperate need to bind and irrevocably mark a woman. Love wasn't a sick feeling in the stomach, was it? Or the terrifying conviction that he had lost all control of his life? The notion that

Dani was becoming *necessary* to him was scary as hell.

She was a decent woman and more honest than any other he had ever known. Her life was an open book. But if he told her even a fraction of what he was feeling, that would give her power over him, the power to destroy.

So he held his tongue, but he showed her with his body. Like a madman, he forced his way between smooth thighs and took her in an agony of longing, as if he would never get enough. As if filling her and finding release was the ultimate calling of his life.

Loving her gently was far easier when the first storm had passed. He stroked curves and valleys, feathering his fingertips across her most sensitive flesh and relishing her ragged cries when he gave her what she needed most.

Holding her afterward was almost as good. With her back pressed to his chest and her bottom cradled against his pelvis, he found peace. Burying his face in her hair, he inhaled her scent and tried to commit it to memory. Nothing this good could last. Nothing ever did.

In the middle of the night, Dani took a turn

waking him. "Hold me," she whispered. "Make love to me again. Christmas is over, and I'm afraid of tomorrow."

He had no assurances to offer. They both knew the score. It added up to messy confusion and ultimately, change. A change he didn't want, but a change that was necessary. The best he could do right now was pretend.

Dani woke up just before 5:00 a.m. and went to the bathroom. Then, with her heart breaking, she stared into the mirror and tried to recognize the woman with the tousled hair and the tired eyes and the whisker burns on her neck.

How could they go forward from here? Nathaniel was never going to change. Dani had too much self-respect to settle for a relationship that was less than a hundred percent. She wanted a normal life.

Nathaniel Winston was not normal in any way. He was brilliant and driven. Generous, but at the same time distant. She knew he cared about her in an academic fashion. Just as he cared about Peaches. That wasn't enough. Dani wanted everything or nothing at all.

Maybe he felt something more for her than a primal, male need to possess. Maybe he could fall in love with her. Was she willing to take that chance? Was she willing to wait for something that might never happen?

Yawning and desolate, she returned to the bedroom and climbed back under the covers. Nathaniel was dead asleep, but when she touched his chest, he mumbled and reached for her, dragging her against him. Dani closed her eyes and fell asleep, wrapped in the bittersweet comfort of ephemeral bliss.

The next time she awoke, the room was filled with light. Nathaniel lay on his side facing her, his head propped on his hand. He looked younger and happier than she had ever seen him. Peaches lay between them, contentedly gumming the edge of the sheet.

Dani rubbed her eyes with the heels of her hands and stretched with a yawn. "Sorry, I must have been out cold."

Nathaniel grinned. "You were indeed. I suppose someone kept you awake most of the night."

His smug, male satisfaction amused her despite

the turmoil in her heart. She twirled one of the baby's curls around her finger. "Naughty baby."

"Very funny." He tangled his hand in Dani's hair and leaned over to kiss her. "I've decided to go to Gainesville with you. If the offer's still open."

"Of course it is. But what about work? What changed your mind?"

"NCT can do without me for one day. We've all three been cooped up since Friday. A road trip sounds like fun. You can tell your brother not to worry about picking you up."

"I hate to burst your bubble, but how exactly are we going to get there? Your Mercedes is in a drugstore parking lot under a mound of snow, and there's still the matter of the car seat."

"Out of curiosity, how did *you* envision us traveling when you first invited me to go with you?"

"Truthfully?" She grimaced. "I thought you would say no immediately, so it was a moot point."

Her answer bothered him. She could see it in his eyes, but he recovered quickly. "Well, I guess the joke is on you. I'm coming, and I've got the

transportation problem solved. I've ordered a vehicle with a regulation car seat already installed."

"A car?"

"A vehicle."

"As in…?"

For a moment, he looked like a kid caught
cheating on his homework. "I requested a Hummer. It will be delivered at four this afternoon."

Dani gaped. "A Hummer? Are you serious?
Why would you do that?"

Nathaniel shrugged. "It's a virtually indestructible vehicle. Look out the window, woman. The
melting has started, but it won't be gone in an
hour. Nobody in Atlanta knows how to drive in
the snow. It's dangerous to be out and about. Besides, all that water has to go somewhere, which
means flooding. Peaches may not be mine, but
I have a responsibility to keep her safe until the
investigator gets some answers. I want to keep
you safe, too."

"And you want to drive a Hummer."

His sheepish grin acknowledged the truth of
her accusation. "Is that so bad?"

"My brother will go nuts. I hope you don't mind

sharing. He'll have the two of you careening all over Hall County."

"There are worse ways to spend an afternoon."

"Good grief." She muttered the words beneath her breath as she got out of bed. At five this morning after visiting the bathroom, she had donned her nightgown before getting back under the covers. Her mental state required some kind of armor, even if it was flimsy silk and even if the silk had been purchased by the man on the other side of the bed. Now she added the robe and belted it. "Shall I fix us some breakfast?"

Every bit of humor left his face. His eyes darkened and his jaw tightened. "What I'd like is for Ophelia to reclaim her baby so I can spend a few more hours in bed with you. Last night was amazing."

"Hush," she said. "Not in front of Peaches."

He stared at her so intently her nipples beaded beneath two thin layers of silk. Nathaniel noticed, of course. "She doesn't understand a thing I'm saying. Nor does she know how badly I want her to take a long, morning nap."

"Stop it, please. You're embarrassing me." Her cheeks felt sunburned. Why did the man in the bed have to be so sexy, so charming, so funny, so *everything*?

"Fine," he said. "Go scramble a few eggs if it will make you happy. But don't expect me to forget about sex. Not after last night."

If Christmas Day had been long and lazy, Monday was anything but. Since the holiday fell on Sunday, most of Atlanta had Monday off, which meant traffic was lighter than usual on the interstates. That helped road crews who were trying desperately to restore order. Unfortunately, even that advantage was negated by the dozens of wrecks all over the city. Dani and Nathaniel took turns listening to the radio, scouring online news sites and occasionally, catching breaking-news updates on TV.

Peaches was inconsolable for most of the day. She did, in fact, have one tiny tooth poking through on the bottom with a second one soon on the way. "No wonder she's cranky," Dani said after lunch. "Poor thing is miserable."

Since they didn't want to get out twice, Dani made a list and Nathaniel placed a phone order to the same pharmacy/discount store where they had first gathered supplies for the baby. This time

Dani included infant acetaminophen and a fluid-filled teething ring that could be frozen. They needed something to comfort the poor child.

While the grown-ups took turns packing overnight bags, the baby slept for no more than ten minutes at a time. Dani, frazzled and exhausted, began to wonder if this trip to Gainesville was a good idea after all. On the other hand, her parents would be crushed if she cancelled at this late date.

Nathaniel loaned her a small suitcase. She managed to get all of the gifts he had given her folded neatly inside. The family lunch would be extremely casual, and she had told Nathaniel as much. The jeans she chose to wear from her new mini wardrobe, however, were superchic, as was the long-sleeve top in shades of purple and mauve and silver. Never had she spent this much money on items that were essentially a knock-around wardrobe.

The outfit must have been flattering, because Nathaniel's eyes narrowed and his neck flushed when he saw her. "You almost ready?" he asked.

Dani nodded, tucking her hair behind her ears.

"I think we're just waiting for the drugstore order and we're good to go."

Nathaniel handed her the baby. "I'm going downstairs to sign for the car. I'll load the delivery straight into the back."

"You won't need all that for one night."

"Doesn't matter. I've got plenty of room in the Hummer."

She laughed. "You love saying that, don't you?"

His wicked smile made her stomach flip. "I don't know *what* you're talking about."

When the front door slammed behind him, Dani nuzzled Peaches's soft cheeks and tried to remember everything she needed to pick up at her apartment. Thanks to Nathaniel's largesse, it was mostly only the presents for her family.

Thirty minutes later, they were on the road. Dani had worried about Peaches's safety, but the car seat was top-of-the-line and installed correctly. The baby settled down once they were in the ridiculously large and noticeable vehicle, perhaps from the novelty of being outside.

The huge amounts of melting snow did indeed create a nightmare. Not only that, but Nathaniel was forced to dodge vehicles that had been abandoned Friday night. The side trip to Dani's apartment took far longer than it should have. She shared the top floor of an old Victorian house in the Piedmont Park area.

"This is nice," Nathaniel said, surveying the tree-lined streets and charming architecture.

"I won't be long at all."

"Don't you need help?"

"No. I'll be fine." She didn't want Nathaniel inside her home, even briefly. It was going to be hard enough to root him out of her life without the memory of his presence inside the one place that was her peaceful sanctuary at the end of a long day.

She was gone fifteen minutes, maybe twenty. "Sorry," she said as she carefully placed the sack of gifts in the back and climbed into the front of the vehicle. "I had to water a couple of plants."

"No worries."

As Nathaniel negotiated the newly created obstacle course to get out of town, Dani texted back and forth with her mother. Finally, she shut off her phone and tossed it in her purse. "I hope we make it to Gainesville and the hotel in one piece."

He shifted into a lower gear to tackle an icy

hill. "We'll make it," he said. "And we'll cele-brate in bed, little elf. Frankly, it's all I'm think-ing about at the moment. That and trying not to smash up this tank I'm driving."

"I thought it wasn't smashable," she quipped, goading him for no good reason.

He scowled as the driver to their right ran a stop sign. "True. It would be more correct to say I'm worried about smashing up all the *other* ve-hicles on the road. Do me a favor and quit talk-ing for now. I need to concentrate."

Normally the drive from Atlanta to Gaines-ville—northeast of the city—took an hour to an hour and half, depending upon time of day. Today, the traffic crawled. All lanes of the inter-state were clear, but stranded vehicles on the side of the road created hazards. Not only that, but the people who hadn't been able to travel Satur-day and Sunday were out in full force, clogging the roads.

When they finally made it to the outskirts of Dani's hometown, she had a tension headache and an empty stomach. Peaches had slept the first hour and cried on and off the rest of the trip. Nathaniel pointed out a popular steak house. "Do you want to stop for dinner before we check in?"

The thought of juggling a cranky baby was daunting. "Would you mind if we ordered pizza and had it delivered to the room?"

"Not at all. I should have thought of that."

The all-suite hotel Dani had chosen was part of a chain, but a nice one. A friendly bellman helped them wrangle all their stuff upstairs and beamed when Nathaniel tipped him generously. The young man wanted to linger and discuss the Hummer's unique features. Dani eased him out the door. "We need to feed the baby. Thanks again for all your help."

Nathaniel collapsed in an armchair and rubbed his temples. "I *never* want to make that drive again."

"Me, either," Dani said, feeling guilty. "I had no idea it would be so bad. I'm sorry I dragged you into this."

He gave her a tired smile that still had enough wattage to curl her toes. "I came along of my own free will. Besides, this may be the only time in my life I can justify the Hummer."

"Was it worth the price?"

"Every penny." He kicked off his shoes. "Let me have the baby, and you order our pizza. I'll eat anything but anchovies. And onions."

"Sounds good."

Often, when Nathaniel decided to work through lunch at NCT, Dani was the one who ordered meals brought in. It wasn't unusual for the two of them to sit together in Nathaniel's office and eat while he kept working and she took notes or sent emails at his request.

Never once in those situations had she ever felt self-conscious or weird. Tonight, every moment felt like new territory.

Fortunately, the local pizza place was close by. Delivery was prompt and efficient. While Dani handled the meal order, Nathaniel gave Peaches a bottle. He was an old pro at it already. Soon, Peaches was asleep. They spread a blanket on the rug near them and put the baby on her tummy. She scrunched her cute little face and drew her knees under her, her bottom tilted upward in her favorite sleep position.

While they consumed the hot, extra cheesy ham-and-pineapple pizza, silence reigned. Dani knew she should come right out and tell Nathaniel she was looking for another job. He would probably be pleased. It would be impossible for things to go back to the way they were at the office. After this bizarre Christmas weekend that was both wonderful and challenging in equal parts, life was going to be very different.

Dani wasn't scheduled to go back to work until January 3. She'd banked the last of her vacation time to give herself a nice, long holiday at the end of the year. Her plans for the remainder of this week were modest: clean out her closet, see a couple of movies she had missed and stock up on groceries to cook healthy, yummy meals for January.

She didn't always make New Year's resolutions, but this time around was different. In the spirit of being proactive, she would schedule herself an appointment on Nathaniel's calendar for that first day back, sit down with him and quit her job face-to-face.

Just thinking of it made her hands clammy and her stomach queasy. The boss was a holy terror when he was mad. Woe to the person who became the focus of his icy cold displeasure. Still, only a coward ended a job *or* a relationship with a note, online or otherwise.

Nathaniel tapped the edge of the box. "You want to share the last piece?"

"It's all yours," she said.

If Nathaniel had even once offered a single shred of evidence that he was thinking about a future for the two of them, she might have found the courage to tell him she loved him. After all, nothing dictated that the man had to be first to lay his heart on the line.

Unfortunately, Nathaniel had done nothing to indicate a desire for permanence.

Which meant that tonight and tomorrow were it.

Without saying a word, he gathered up the empty pizza box and the paper plates and napkins, and carried them out to the trash chute in the hall. When he returned, he lifted an eyebrow. "What's wrong, Christmas elf? I've never seen you bite your fingernails."

She jerked her hand away from her mouth. "Nothing's wrong," she lied. "I might be a tiny bit nervous about tomorrow, that's all."

They had been sitting on the floor with their

backs against the sofa. He dropped down beside her and put a hand on her knee. "Peaches and I can always stay here. Your brother could pick you up and bring you back."

"I want you to come," she said slowly. "I just don't want anybody getting stupid ideas about you and me."

It was the perfect opening for him to make a suggestive remark, or even admit he wouldn't think that was a terrible idea if it happened.

Nathaniel did neither.

Instead, he picked up his phone and began looking at emails. "I thought I would hear something from the investigator by now."

Dani swallowed her disappointment and hurt. It wasn't Nathaniel's fault she'd been weaving fantasies. She stood and crossed the room to put some distance between them. "Did he say how he would start his search?"

"I imagine he'll follow the credit card trail. That seems to be the easiest route."

"Except if Ophelia got stuck in one place like we were, there might be no credit card activity to find."

"True. But even if that were so, I'm betting

today is different. As soon as transactions start popping up, he'll find her."

"I hope so." She crouched beside the baby, already half in love with Peaches herself. "She's so sweet and good-natured. I hope that means Ophelia is a good mother most of the time."

Nathaniel's expression darkened. "I didn't have much of a mother at all, but I turned out okay, didn't I?"

"Of course," Dani said lightly. *If you don't count the fact that you're distrustful of women in general and emotionally closed off to a clinical degree.* "I think there are a couple of bowl games on. If you want to watch them, I'll read for a while. I grabbed a book when I ran up to the apartment."

"You don't mind?"

"Not at all."

The tension between them was impossible to ignore. Big emotions were at stake, but Nathaniel *wouldn't* talk about them, and Dani couldn't. The result was an uneasy truce.

Peaches woke up after an hour. The atmosphere in the hotel room eased after that. The baby provided not only a center point for conversation, but plenty of hands-on work to keep them busy.

At almost ten, Nathaniel's cell phone dinged. His expression was triumphant as he read the text. He looked up at Dani with a grim smile. "She bought gas and groceries in Decatur."

"That's good, then—right? She's still in town?"

"Unless she's headed north to run away."

"Don't think like that," Dani said. "Being the mother of an infant is stressful and emotionally draining. I'll bet Ophelia had a freak-out moment for some reason, and she brought the baby to you. Once she gets her head on straight, she'll want Peaches back again."

"Let's hope so."

Their little charge went out for the night not long after that. Dani showered and put on the ivory gown and robe. The king-size bed in the center of the room was an invitation for romantic sex, or so it seemed to Dani's heated longings.

As if he had read her mind, Nathaniel crossed the space separating them and moved behind her, linking his arms around her waist. He rested his chin on top of her head. "I hope you're ready for bed," he said.

"I *am* pretty tired."

He spun her around to face him and bent to stare into her eyes. "Please tell me that was a joke. I should get stars in my crown for keeping my hands off you all day."

"You were too busy with the traffic to notice me."

"Don't fish for compliments, elf. I'm obsessed with you, and it's damned uncomfortable."

Ten

Nathaniel had never meant to be so honest. But his moments with Dani were slipping away. He couldn't afford to waste a single one.

Tonight seemed like an ending—bittersweet and momentous at the same time. He was damned tempted not to let her go. Her openness and caring were the antithesis of the way he lived his life. Keeping her would be not only dangerous, but selfish. He couldn't imagine a future without her, but he *knew* he wasn't equipped to be the man she needed.

He undressed her carefully and then removed the athletic pants he had donned after his shower.

They climbed into bed without speaking. He pulled her to the center of the mattress and wrapped his arms around her. "I don't want to hurt you, Dani."

Dani went rigid in his embrace. "I can take care of myself," she said, the words tart. "Maybe you should worry about *me* hurting you."

He smiled in the darkness. She was reminding him that their relationship was a two-way street. What she couldn't know was that he had gone years without letting women get close enough to penetrate the walls around his heart. If anyone had the power, it would have been Dani. But he was in no danger. He held all the cards.

As long as he remained in control, everything would go according to plan. He could assign Dani to a new division and gradually wean himself from her allure.

He hadn't allowed himself to fall in love with her. That was how he knew everything was going to be okay.

For the next hour, he lost himself in the pleasure of her body. The sex was as good as it had ever been, but something was a little off. His Christmas elf wasn't as open with him as before.

She held something back. Put up a few no-trespassing signs.

Her reticence might have been infuriating if he hadn't been balls deep in making love to her. Not *loving* her. There was a difference.

Each time he made her come, he was jubilant. She might have other lovers after him, but he was determined she wouldn't be able to erase the memories of tonight.

Beyond that testosterone-fueled goal lingered a strange mixture of elation and terror. His body was sated, lax with bone-deep pleasure. He held Dani close and buried his face in her hair.

It was only sex, he told himself desperately. Only sex…

Morning came far too soon. Peaches had given them a good six-hour stretch, taken a bottle and then gone right back to sleep until almost eight o'clock. Even so, Nathaniel wanted to spend the morning in bed. With Dani.

As they took turns getting ready, his lover was quiet. It was just as well. He had nothing witty to say, no funny quips about melting snow or holiday blues or poopy diapers.

Dani's mother was preparing Christmas lunch for the midday meal. Dani and Nathaniel were instructed to arrive no later than eleven in order to have time for opening presents and taking official family photos.

The Meadows family owned fifteen acres of land outside of town. Their property ran alongside a rich river bottom and up the side of a small hill. Dani had told him stories about running barefoot through fields of cotton and catching fireflies on hot summer nights.

He was charmed in spite of himself. Such rustic, simple pleasures were a million miles away from his own upbringing. Oftentimes as a kid, he'd spent hours at the kitchen table, figuring out homework on his own and listening to the ticking of the mantel clock as it echoed in their elegant, lonely home.

Shaking off the maudlin thoughts, he concentrated on maneuvering the Hummer around Gainesville. "Nice town," he said.

"It was a fun place to grow up. I love Atlanta, though. I'm a big-city girl at heart. I even thought about moving to New York at one time."

"But?"

"It's expensive. And I would miss my family. Atlanta is home."

At a red light, he braked and glanced in the rearview mirror. "Is she doing okay?"

"Almost asleep. I wish we could drive around long enough for her get a good nap. Mom expects promptness, though. My siblings and I learned that the hard way. If we came in late from a date or a party, we'd be grounded for two weeks. It was effective punishment."

"Don't take this wrong, but it sounds like the Meadowses are a typical American family. It's nice."

Dani shrugged. "You could say that. Still, even typical American families have problems, Nathaniel. Normalcy doesn't exempt anyone from pain and tragedy."

He mulled over her odd answer as they drove ever closer to Dani's childhood home. Was she trying to tell him something, or was he reading too much into her words?

When they finally made it to the other side of town and out into the country, Nathaniel thought they were home free. The sky was gray and the trees bare, but it was warm—fifty degrees already. He hadn't counted on the scenic creek that ran through the Meadowses' property.

To ascend the drive that led to the house, it was necessary to cross the creek on a narrow concrete bridge. Today, the creek was a raging river...and rising rapidly.

Dani's hands gripped the dash and the door, white-knuckle. "I don't like this, Nathaniel."

"Hummers were meant for situations like today," he said. "There's barely any water over the bridge yet, so I'll take it slow and we'll be fine."

They inched their way forward. The water was still rising, but certainly not fast enough to sweep the Hummer off the bridge. For a brief moment, it occurred to him he might be getting stuck with Dani in another weather-related situation, but he ignored the thought. He tightened his grip on the wheel and pressed the gas pedal carefully.

The vehicle kept a gratifying grip on the road surface. "See," he said. "You were worried about nothing."

In the next second, he saw a large section of creek bank in front of them crumble into the muddy water. With a loud, groaning *crack*, a corner of the concrete bridge gave in to forces it was never meant to withstand.

"Hold on," Nathaniel yelled. They were six feet from safety. More of the concrete could give way at any moment. He gunned the engine, floored the gas pedal and made the unwieldy vehicle lurch forward like an elephant released from a slingshot.

Everything happened in slow motion. Dani screamed. Another chunk of the bridge sheared off. But the Hummer came through for him. They landed on firm ground, inches away from the disaster they had so narrowly missed.

He shifted into Park with a shaky hand and reached for Dani. "God, I'm sorry. Are you okay?" They glanced at the back seat in unison, reassuring themselves that the baby had slept through it all.

Dani nodded, her face milk white. "I'm fine. It wasn't your fault."

It was, and he would kick himself for that later, but now all he wanted to do was reassure himself they were alive. He cupped Dani's head in two hands and turned her face up to his for a frantic kiss. His heart still beat in sickening thuds. "Your parents will shoot me," he said hoarsely.

Dani's arms were wrapped so tightly around his neck she threatened to strangle him. It didn't matter. The fragrance of her skin and the tremors that shook her body were killing him bit by bit with guilt. She might have been hurt. He could have lost her.

"We're fine," she insisted, though it was clear she couldn't stop shaking. "You saved us, Nathaniel. If we'd been on that bridge and it collapsed, we could have ended up nose first in the water. I don't even want to think about it."

"Me, either," he said. He rested his forehead against hers. "Damn it, little elf, I nearly ruined your storybook Christmas."

She laughed softly, her fingertips caressing the hair at his nape and making him shiver. "There was never anything storybook about this holiday. I suppose today is more of the same. Come on. Let's go get some lunch. Adrenaline makes me hungry."

Dani moved through the next hours in a dream. She'd done her best to reassure Nathaniel that their near disaster wasn't his fault. The experience shook her to the core. Personal danger wasn't at the heart of it. What if Peaches had come to harm? Or Nathaniel?

The terrifying moments on the bridge replayed in slow motion in her brain, even as she greeted her family and introduced Nathaniel and Peaches all around. It had been a long time since the Meadows clan had an infant in the house, so the baby helped defuse any awkwardness about Nathaniel's presence.

Nathaniel himself rolled out a generous helping of charm, complimenting Dani's parents on their home and their view. Lunch was delayed when the men decided they needed to check the status of the rising creek. The four males donned rain boots—some borrowed—and trudged down to the bottom of the hill while Dani and her mom and sister put the finishing touches on the meal.

Dani held the baby and snitched a piece of ham. "This looks amazing, Mom. You must have been up since dawn."

"Angie helped a lot. Why don't we go hang out in the den until the boys get back? No sense standing when we can sit."

Dani knew what was coming next. Jared hadn't brought a date. With only her mother and sister in the room, the confrontation to come was a given.

Angie played leadoff. "So tell me, little sis. Since when are you and the head of NCT so chummy?"

"I explained that already. It was a weird situation. He was going to drive me to the train station, but the snow got too bad too fast."

"And that's when you found the baby." Angie rolled her eyes. "Give me a break. This sounds like an episode of a really bad soap opera."

Dani's mother intervened. "Don't be rude to your sister, Angie." She pinned Dani with the kind of look parents perfect when their kids are still toddlers. "Are you sleeping with him?"

"Mom!" Mortification flooded Dani's face with heat.

"That's not an answer."

"He's my boss," Dani said, desperately wishing she had never initiated the idea of Nathaniel coming with her. "That would be entirely inappropriate."

"Danielle…" Her mother's voice went up an octave.

Dani clutched Peaches and straightened her spine. "There's nothing going on between us. Nathaniel doesn't trust women. He's a confirmed bachelor."

Angie pointed across the room, sympathy on her face. "Too late, kid. Give it up. Mom was worried about the creek. She and Dad have been scouring the valley all morning."

Dani looked over at the cushioned seat in the bay window. There were the high-end binoculars she had bought her dad last Christmas. For birdwatching. "Oh?"

Her sister put an arm around her waist and leaned in to whisper in her ear. "They saw the kiss, Dani. Every passionate second. You're busted."

"I can explain. We were scared. It was adrenaline."

Her mother frowned. "Is this serious, Dani?"

"No," she cried. "I swear it's not. Please don't make a big deal about nothing."

Fortunately, the men returned before her mother could continue the inquisition. Dani was temporarily saved from further embarrassment. Everyone was hungry, so presents had to wait.

Over lunch, the adults teased each other with old stories about Christmases past. The year Jared opened all his presents in the middle of the night and tried to rewrap them before morning. The time Angie cried when she didn't get a doll she had actually forgotten to ask Santa for. And then Dani's most embarrassing Christmas. The one when her high-school boyfriend gave her a kitten because he didn't know she was allergic.

Jared finished the tale. "Oh, man, Nathaniel, you should have seen Dani. She was covered in red welts from head to toe. It was the quickest breakup in the history of teenage dating."

Nathaniel grinned. "It's hard to imagine. The Dani I know at work never gets flustered by anything."

"Okay," Dani said. "Enough family stories. Pass the sweet potatoes, please. Mom, why don't you and Dad tell Nathaniel about your trip to Hong Kong last summer."

Nathaniel was actually having fun. He had expected to sit back as a spectator while Dani enjoyed holiday rituals with her family. Instead, he had been pulled into the fray with a vengeance.

The Meadows clan swapped jokes and debated blockbuster movies and argued politics passionately, including Nathaniel at every turn.

The only subject completely off-limits was Peaches. He knew Dani had explained the bare bones of the situation. Dani's siblings and parents handled the baby's presence with sensitivity. They didn't ignore her, but they also didn't say or do anything to make Nathaniel feel uncomfortable.

In the unlikely situation in which he found himself, his hosts' kindness and generosity were extraordinary. "May I propose a toast?" he asked as Mrs. Meadows brought out a ten-layer apple stack cake and a bowl of freshly whipped cream.

"Of course," Jared said. "But do it quick—before we all fall asleep. The tryptophan in the turkey is doing a number on me."

Nathaniel raised his glass of wine. "To snowstorms and spontaneity and hospitable families. Thanks for including me."

"Hear, hear," Dani's father said. "Now, about that Hummer…"

As Jared and his father argued over who would get first turn behind the wheel, Nathaniel followed Dani into the den where a mound of beautifully wrapped presents was piled beneath a real Fraser fir Christmas tree. The room smelled amazing, a cross between Alpine ski weekends and the comfort of home.

For a moment, Nathaniel felt a keen sense of loss for something he had never known in the first place. Shaking off the odd feeling, he took the baby from Dani. "You've been holding her forever. My turn, I think."

It was eye-opening to watch how the siblings and Dani's parents related to her. At New Century Tech, Nathaniel knew Dani as sharp and capable and goal oriented. In this setting, she was the "baby" of the crew. They petted her and teased her. Perhaps it was so ingrained in the family dynamic they didn't realize how much they underestimated her.

Nathaniel had done nearly the same on a more personal level. At work, he kept such rigid boundaries he never allowed himself to fully appreciate Dani's qualities as a woman, though the physical awareness had been there all along. It had taken a massive snowstorm to make him see what he was missing.

Dani was funny and warm and sexy. Brains and beauty in one appealing package.

Not for the world would he have embarrassed her in front of her family. Despite his hunger to be with her, he kept his distance physically, never touching her arm or tucking her hair behind her ear. He and Dani played the role of business associates perfectly. No one would ever guess they had spent the weekend making love at every turn.

He was touched and surprised to know that Dani's mother had somehow found a couple of things to wrap for *him*. He opened a navy-and-burgundy silk tie and a pair of sterling silver cuff links.

In the midst of the pandemonium of wrapping paper and boxes and bows, Nathaniel found himself trying to imagine what it would be like if he were a real member of this family. Heart pounding in his chest, he looked across the room at Dani and found her gaze on him. Her beautiful blue eyes shone bright with happiness.

The truth hit him without warning. A tsunami of feelings tightened his throat and glazed his eyes with moisture. He loved her. He was in love with his executive assistant.

This was a hell of a time for a personal epiphany. His head spun. The conversation swirled around him. He must have participated in appropriate ways, but he felt clumsy, his faculties impaired.

"Excuse me," he said, when he could form the words. "Peaches wants her bottle. I'll be right back."

He fled the family celebration. In the kitchen, he clutched the baby and searched for the premixed bottles of formula Dani had ordered, the same kind they had used that first night. With shaking hands, he uncapped and heated and tested. The routine was not so intimidating now. Against all odds, he was learning how to deal with a baby.

Once the bottle was ready, he went in search of a quiet bedroom. The house was very nice, but not all that large. Even with the door closed, he could hear echoes of the festivities from down the hall. He sat on the edge of the bed and cradled the little girl in his arms. She smiled up at him as she gripped the bottle.

Damn it. Dani was right. He didn't want the complicated situation, but it was going to break his heart if she weren't his flesh and blood.

Females were trouble. That was the truth. How was he going to let either one of them go?

Immediately after the formula was gone, Peaches fell sound asleep. He tugged the bottle from her hands and set it aside. Carefully, he lifted the small, limp body onto his shoulder.

He wanted to be alone. He needed time and space to process everything that was happening to him. Unfortunately, he was smack-dab in the middle of a good old-fashioned family Christmas.

When he made it back to the den, Jared cornered him. "It's not going to be safe to get across that bridge. At least not until the water goes down and Dad and I can see how much damage was done. There's an alternate route off the back side of the property, but it will add almost an hour to your trip."

Dani's mother joined them. "I know we're crowded, but I would feel better if you stayed the night, Nathaniel. I don't want you taking my daughter and the baby across the bridge today, Hummer or no Hummer. And that other road is terrible. We have all sorts of blankets and sleeping bags, more than enough to make comfy pallets here in front of the fire. I thought about kicking Jared out of his room, but his is a twin bed, so not much help."

Nathaniel swallowed his misgivings. "Dani can have the sofa. I'd be happy to stay, Mrs. Meadows, but I definitely will have to get on the road first thing in the morning to make it back to work."

"Of course," Dani's mother said. She turned around and looked at her daughter. "You don't mind camping out for just one night, do you, sweetheart?"

Dani had a deer-in-the-headlights look. "It's okay with me, Mama, if Nathaniel agrees."

Mrs. Meadows beamed. "Then it's settled."

For Nathaniel, the torture was only beginning. His plan had been to leave around four in the afternoon and hightail it back to Atlanta. He would drop Dani off at her apartment, and he and Peaches would go to his condo to wait for Ophelia.

Now he was going to spend another night with the woman he wanted more than his next breath.

In her parents' house. With a baby as chaperone. God help him. It was everything he feared and everything he couldn't have.

The warm, loving family, the precious baby, the woman who tempted him beyond reason. How could he keep a rein on his hunger if the two of them were trapped in this house?

Despite his inner turmoil, the day passed quickly. As Dani had warned, the men were eager to try out the Hummer. Even Angie's husband went along for the excursion across snow-covered fields.

Nathaniel enjoyed the outing far more than he expected. Angie's husband possessed a dry wit. Dani's father turned out to be a good old country boy at heart and Jared was, as Dani had told him, brilliant. The four men took turns behind the wheel, tackling hills and whooping it up when the Hummer conquered all obstacles.

Before returning home, they went as close as they dared to the raging creek and assessed the conditions. According to the National Weather Service, the rising waters had finally peaked. With no rain in the forecast and only the melting snow to feed the torrent, the outlook was good.

By morning it was possible that the usually placid brook might be near normal levels.

Back at the house, the women had whipped up another batch of mouthwatering food for dinner. Nathaniel was amazed the whole family managed to stay fit and trim. Maybe they burned it off because no one ever sat still.

The evening was devoted to charades and card games. Nathaniel cleaned up at poker but was lousy at charades. Even Angie's husband, the other outsider, was better at guessing clues than Nathaniel. They all teased him, but it was good-natured.

How could he tell them his focus was shot to hell because he was fixated on the prospect of another night with Dani?

At long last, the day drew to a close. One by one, family members disappeared to shower and get ready for bed. Dani's father dragged out all the extra bedding and helped make a comfortable sleeping spot for Nathaniel and Peaches. Dani tucked a sheet around the sofa cushions and added a blanket.

"We'll be fine, Dad. Thanks for everything."

Nathaniel nodded. "Thank you, sir. It was a great day."

Was it his imagination, or did Dani's father give him the stink eye before walking out of the room? Then it dawned on Nathaniel. The den had no door. A double doorway, yes. But no way to secure privacy with lock and key. *Hell's bells.*

Dani didn't bother with the nightwear he had bought for her. She was wearing borrowed sweatpants from her sister, topped with an Atlanta Braves T-shirt. With her hair up in a ponytail, she could have passed for a teenager.

Nathaniel excused himself for a turn in the bathroom. He opted for soft athletic pants and a thin cotton shirt, leaving it unbuttoned in deference to the fact that the fire made the den *very* toasty. They wouldn't have to worry about Peaches getting cold.

When he returned, Dani had turned out all the lights. She was tucked into her temporary bed on the sofa with the covers pulled up to her chin. She had taken the rubber band out of her hair, and now the thick, caramel tresses fanned out across her pillow in an appealing tumble. Her eyes were closed, but he'd bet a thousand dollars she was wide awake.

Peaches was asleep in her usual position.

He sat down on the end of the sofa and put Dani's feet in his lap.

She opened one eye. "I just got comfortable," she complained. "Shouldn't we get some sleep if we're getting up early?"

"It's ten thirty," he pointed out. "You and I are usually good for another several hours at this point. You know, when things get cranked up."

Her gaze was wild. "Nathaniel! Hush! Are you out of your mind? Somebody could be standing outside in the hall listening to us."

"They're not. I checked." He slipped his hand under the covers and played with her ankle bone. "I've barely touched you all day."

Eleven

Dani moaned. With Nathaniel's thumb pressing into the arch of her foot, her whole body turned to honey. "We can't," she muttered. "Somebody might come in."

"You don't think they'll give us privacy?"

"Yes. No. I don't know." He ran his hand up her calf but stopped at her knee. She wanted him so badly she was shaking. But this situation was fraught with impossibility.

Nathaniel nodded soberly. In the firelight, she could swear his eyes danced with mischief. "I understand. You think this is a bad idea. No worries. I'll read a book on my iPad and let you sleep."

When he started to stand up, Dani grabbed his wrist. "We'll have to be very quiet," she said, caving in to the yearning that made her abandon caution in favor of gratification.

Nathaniel looked shocked. "You're serious? I was kidding, Dani. I assumed fooling around was out of the question. You know, under the circumstances."

She sat up and raked the hair away from her face. "I need you," she said, searching his face to see if he felt even a fraction of the urgency that tore her apart. Need and want and every nuanced shading in between. She loved him. Greedily, she would snatch every possible opportunity to be with him.

"I won't say no to you, elf. How could I?"

He dragged her into his arms and kissed her softly, his fingers winnowing through her tangled hair. His breathing was not quite steady. That reassured Dani on some level. She didn't want to be the only one flying blind—jumping without a net—indulging without weighing the consequences.

Carefully, tenderly, he eased her down onto the carpet and slid both his hands under her shirt.

When he cupped her breasts and thumbed her nipples, she had to bite down hard on her lower lip to keep from crying out.

The need for silence was frustrating, but it lent a titillating touch of danger. She cupped his face in her hands. He hadn't shaved. His jaw was covered in masculine stubble. "I'm glad you're here," she whispered.

"Me, too."

After that, there was not much need for words. The fire popped and crackled. Occasionally the baby made tiny noises in her sleep. Nathaniel slid Dani's pants and panties down her legs and removed them. With her shirt rucked up to her armpits, she was essentially naked. He stared her as if he had never seen her before, or maybe he had never seen a *woman* before. That's how wild and reckless and incredulous he seemed.

He freed his sex and found a condom. Seconds later he spread her thighs and thrust roughly, pinning her wrists above her head with one big hand. "I don't know what to do about you, elf. Tell me. Can anything this good last?"

When she didn't answer, his jaw hardened. What did he expect? What did he want from her? It was a rhetorical question as far as Dani could tell.

Nathaniel's big body was warm and hard against hers. He took her forcefully at first and then tauntingly slow in the next minute. Dani unraveled rapidly. With her hands bound, she felt helpless. At his mercy. His masculine scent surrounded her, making her crazy.

"Ah, damn," he groaned. His entire body went rigid. His chest radiated heat. His hips pinned her to the floor. He kissed her with bruising demand.

Rolling onto his side and moving her with him, he took advantage of the new position and touched her sex intimately. Heartbeats later, Dani came.

He covered her mouth with one large hand to smother her cry. Then he shoved her onto her back again and pummeled wildly until he buried his face in her neck and came for long, stormy seconds.

Dani dozed in Nathaniel's embrace until she found the strength to drag herself back to reality. Her body was relaxed and sated, but her heart ached with a throb that frightened her. She didn't want to love Nathaniel like this. She hated feeling so vulnerable. Most of all, she was terrified that sooner rather than later she was going to have to live through the end of whatever this thing was between them.

Affair. Fling. Momentary insanity. Any description she chose sounded temporary and ultimately painful.

Nathaniel roused finally and yawned. "Damn, elf. You're killing me."

She managed a smile. "I don't see you complaining."

"Probably because I'm not an idiot. If a man has to die, there are worse ways to go."

Their lighthearted teasing was a cover for deeper, darker emotions. Nathaniel had to know the end was in sight. She'd told him flat out she wouldn't expect more.

At any point in the past few days he'd had ample opportunity to declare his undying love and beg her to marry him. *That* hadn't happened. He'd done nothing that could be construed as leading her on. Their sexual romp was on her and her alone. She'd made a choice. Now she had to live with the consequences.

"We should get dressed," she said.

"Yeah." His yawn cracked his jaw.

"I hope the creek will be down far enough in the morning. I know you don't want to miss work."

"Doesn't matter," he said. "I called and arranged for a helicopter to pick us up. Jared has offered to return the Hummer to Atlanta for me. If you're afraid to fly, Peaches and I will go without you and you can come with your brother in a day or two."

Was that what he wanted? A clean break?

She swallowed hard. "I don't mind flying. I've never been in a helicopter, though." Men like Nathaniel Winston did things like that. Private jets. Corporate choppers. Once again, the vast gulf between their worlds mocked her.

"You'll like it, I think. Once you catch your breath."

"Sounds fun."

She eluded his embrace and pulled on her clothes. "I need to go to the bathroom."

When she returned, Nathaniel was standing in front of the fire, his back to her. One hand rested on the mantel. The other was shoved in his back pocket. What was he thinking? Poor man. He didn't celebrate Christmas, and yet here he was, neck deep in a Meadows family holiday.

She touched him on the shoulder. "Good night."

He whirled around as if she had startled him, as if he had been lost in thought. He nodded, his expression hooded. "Sleep well, elf." He kissed her gently on the lips.

Dani held back stupid tears. "You, too."

Surprisingly, the night passed without incident. Peaches didn't wake up at all, perhaps worn out from all the extra attention. When the baby finally roused at seven, Dani and Nathaniel were already dressed.

Her mom and dad were early risers. Angie and her husband were still asleep. Jared wouldn't surface until ten at least. He took his days off seriously. It was only the four other adults in the kitchen drinking coffee as the baby took her bottle.

Dani's mom held out her arms. "May I hold her? It's been far too long since we've had a baby in the house. I thought I would have grandchildren by now."

Nathaniel ignored the verbal bait. Dani flushed. Her father sipped his coffee and smiled placidly.

They dined well on apple cake and hot, crispy bacon with fluffy scrambled eggs. Eventually, Nathaniel dabbed his lips with his napkin and glanced at his watch. "We'd better make sure the bags are ready. Won't be long now. Thank you both, for everything."

Dani's mother smiled. "We're so glad you could visit, Nathaniel. I was very sorry to hear Dani will be leaving NCT. I know she has learned so much from you."

The split second of silence was like the sizzle of ozone in the wake of a lightning strike. Nathaniel flinched, his expression blank with shock.

Perhaps Dani was the only one who noticed. He recovered so rapidly, she was stunned. When he looked at her, his gaze was bleak. "Dani has many talents, Mrs. Meadows. I'm sure she'll land on her feet."

He strode out of the room.

Dani followed on his heels, grabbed his arm in the hallway and tried to halt his progress. She might as well have attempted to hold back the ocean. He jerked free, his big, masculine frame rigid.

"I was going to tell you," she said. The explanation sounded weak even to her own ears. "After the holidays. When things settled down."

He seized her wrist in a bruising grasp and dragged her into the hall bathroom, the only place they could be sure of a private moment. When the door was locked behind them, he dropped her hand abruptly as if he couldn't bear to touch her.

"Tell me now," he said coldly. "Tell me the pay was unfair. Tell me I worked you too hard. Tell me I was a sucky boss."

"That's not why," she said, trying to swallow against the giant lump in her throat. "You know it was none of those things. It was this." She cupped his cheek with her hand. "I couldn't stay, because I knew sooner or later you would realize I wanted you. I never dreamed we would end up in bed together," she whispered, willing him to understand.

He stepped backward, forcing her hand to fall, and wrapped his arms around his chest, staring at her with an inscrutable expression. "Do other people at NCT know?"

"Of course not. I thought about telling you this weekend, but I didn't want to ruin things. It was Christmas, not the time to talk about business."

His tight smile made her stomach hurt. "You forget, Dani. I *am* my business." Then he waved a hand sharply as if consigning her to the trash bin. "No matter. I'll make this easy for you. I accept your resignation. I'll have someone pack up the personal items in your desk and deliver them to you next week."

"Nathaniel." She said his name softly—desperately—searching for the right words. "I didn't do anything wrong. You're overreacting. I'm sorry I didn't talk to you sooner. But honestly, this was going to happen anyway. You know I can't work for you anymore." She sucked in a ragged breath. "I care about you."

"Do you? Do you really?" His sarcasm was drenched in ice. "Or is this a female ploy to bring me to my knees?"

"That's not fair." Tears clogged her throat.

With a careless grasp, he took her chin and tipped it upward so they were eye to eye. What destroyed her most was the bleak misery beneath his supercilious glare. Against all odds, she had hurt him deeply, it seemed. "Life's not fair, elf. I learned that a long time ago."

She made the mistake of trying one more time. "I'll go back on the chopper with you. We can talk later today. You need my help with the baby, surely."

Every human emotion inside him shut down as if someone had flipped a switch. His smile chilled her. "On the contrary, Dani. I think I can manage just fine on my own."

Stepping around her, he unlocked the door and walked away.

Watching Nathaniel take Peaches and climb into a fragile-looking helicopter was the worst moment of Dani's life. The rotors hummed with a high-pitched shriek. Wild air currents stirred up leaves and other debris. Moments later, the chopper lifted straight into the air and headed south.

Dani couldn't break down. Not in front of her family. "I'm going for a walk," she muttered. "I'll be back for lunch."

Before either of her parents could say a word of protest, she took off for the hill at the back of the house. The chopper had landed on the only flat spot just behind her father's work shed. Now Dani hurtled down the incline, slipping and stumbling, falling to her knees more than once but getting up again and running. Running.

The pain in her chest was unbearable. She couldn't breathe. She couldn't think.

Why hadn't she talked to him about leaving? Surely he would have understood her decision if he hadn't been blindsided. Hell, he probably would have applauded it. Nathaniel Winston didn't want any messy personal situations to derail his perfectly ordered life.

At last, she came to the copse of trees where she'd passed many a childhood afternoon. On balmy summer nights, she and her siblings had occasionally been allowed to sleep out under the stars in rope hammocks—with their father close at hand, of course.

Today, all the tree limbs were barren, the ground below soggy and muddy from the melting snow. Barely conscious of what she was doing, she jumped for a familiar branch and hauled herself up to sit with her legs dangling. Propping her back against the tree trunk, she put her hands to her face and sobbed.

There was no one around to hear. A hawk soared high above on wind currents. The sun's weak rays provided little warmth. She cried forever it seemed, unconsciously scanning the sky between her fingers, hoping to see the helicopter's return.

Everything was ruined. Even if she found the courage now to tell Nathaniel she loved him, he would question her motives. Distrust and cynicism were deeply ingrained in his personality. She understood why, but understanding didn't make it any easier.

Adding to her distress was the knowledge she would never see the baby again, either. She had hoped to be a support for Nathaniel when everything with Ophelia began to shake out. Either way—father or not the father—Nathaniel would need help sorting through his feelings.

Eventually, she became so cold she knew she had to go inside or risk serious consequences. Her fingers were stiff and numb. She lost her grip getting down from the tree and fell on her face, knocking the wind out of her chest and scratching her chin.

Somehow, the pain seemed appropriate.

The uphill return trip to the house was far longer and more difficult than the flight down. With her head bowed and her eyes wet with tears, she concentrated on not throwing up the breakfast she had eaten earlier.

Jared met her halfway back. She never even saw him coming until he was right in front of her.

He took off his coat and wrapped it around her. "You okay, sis?"

She must have looked dreadful, because her brother's gaze was a mix of concern and alarm. "I will be." It was a promise to herself as well as the answer to his question, but a vow she had no idea how to keep.

Jared put an arm around her waist as they climbed. "I'm gonna go out on a limb here and guess that Nathaniel Winston is more than your boss. Am I right?"

She wiped her nose with the back of her hand. "Yes." Then the truth hit her. "No. Not anymore." The tears came again and with them the certainty that she had derailed her life completely. "I didn't want to fall in love with him, so I began sending out résumés, looking for another job. I was going to tell him soon…about the résumés, not the love thing, but then Mom let the cat out of the bag and now he's furious."

Stumbling to a halt, barely able to catch her breath at the crest of the steep incline, she shivered uncontrollably.

Jared took her by the shoulders and gave her a little shake. "You can't go into the house like this. Mom will freak out. Stay in the shed while I see if the coast is clear."

"Okay."

He was back in under two minutes. "The rest of them are playing cards in the den. If we're quiet, we can slip in the back door and make it to my room. I already grabbed your suitcase."

"Thank you," she whispered.

Jared hesitated. "What are you going to do, Dani?"

She sniffed, wrapping her arms around her waist to keep from flying apart. "I want to go back to Atlanta—right now. I need to talk to him. Will you take me?"

"If we can get the Hummer across the bridge, yes."

"Mom and Dad must be wondering why I didn't get on the helicopter."

"They're smart people. I'm pretty sure they've figured it out by now. Mom feels awful, by the way."

"It wasn't her fault. I never said the job search was a secret."

"Are you positive it wouldn't be better to let this be the end? When only one person is in love, things can get ugly."

"You should know." She managed a teasing tone though she had never felt less like laughing. "Nathaniel doesn't love me. It's true. He won't let himself love anyone. But I *have* been important to him, and I hurt him, I think. I need to apologize. I need closure. So I can move on."

"What if he won't see you?"

She hadn't thought of that. "He will," she said. "I won't give up."

After a restorative hot shower and wearing another set of the clothing Nathaniel had bought for her, Dani found a measure of calm. The conversation with her parents was awkward, but necessary. Though she never mentioned the affair in so many words, it was clear they understood what she had done. They didn't ask questions. It couldn't be easy for a father to think about his daughter having sex.

She spoke with Angie separately and a bit more honestly.

Angie hugged her. "I've had my share of screw-ups, baby sister. You'll survive this, I swear. Call me day or night. I'll even come to Atlanta if you need me."

"Thank you, Angie. I appreciate it."

After that, it was goodbyes all around, and then time to go. While Dani and Angie were having their heart-to-heart, the men had been down to the creek and decided it was safe to traverse the bridge. Though two small sections of concrete were missing, the rest of the structure was sound.

Dani's mom was worried, but Jared kissed her cheek. "I won't do anything stupid, I swear. We'll be fine."

In the end, crossing the bridge was anticlimactic.

Once they negotiated the streets of Gainesville and made it to the other side of town, Jared turned on the radio. The two of them didn't talk, but the lack of conversation was comfortable. He was her brother. He was on her side.

The trip went smoothly. When Jared finally parked the Hummer in front of the building that housed her apartment, he rested an arm on the steering wheel, and turned to face her. "You want me to come in?"

"Not necessary. Thanks for the ride and thanks for returning the Hummer."

His broad grin was cheeky. "I might take it for a little spin before I swing by the car place."

"Jared," she warned, frowning at him.

"Unlimited mileage. I read the contract. As long as I have it there by five o'clock, it's all good."

"You're impossible."

"But you love me."

"Yes, I do." She leaned over and kissed his cheek. "Thanks for everything."

"Do you mind a word of advice?"

"When has that ever stopped you?" It was a rhetorical question.

Jared grimaced. "I'm a guy, Dani. I know how guys think. Sometimes we have to process things. I think you'd be wise to give Winston a few days to cool off. He'll calm down. He'll realize you weren't keeping him in the dark on purpose. If you try to have a confrontation today, things might get even worse."

"I'll think about it," she promised, jumping down from her seat and retrieving her things. She stood on the sidewalk long enough to watch him drive away. The she picked up her suitcase and trudged up the flagstone path to the house.

Twelve

Nathaniel had woefully underestimated how difficult it was going to be to have Peaches at work with him, even for a little while. To make matters worse, Dani's empty office mocked him at every turn. He'd called a temp agency to hire a nanny for the day, but they had no one available except a college student with no real experience in childcare.

Because he was desperate, he told them to send her over. The girl, Wendy, was fine with the baby, careful and attentive to Nathaniel's instructions, but Wendy was a talker. By midafternoon, Nathaniel's patience was shot.

He desperately needed two files Dani had been working on before the holidays. Both were spreadsheets containing customer information. He found the emails where Dani had sent him an original draft, but the contact info he needed was more recent. Unfortunately, he didn't know the passwords for his executive assistant's computer.

A tension headache wrapped his skull in pain. *Get over it, Nathaniel. This is your new reality.* No Dani. No smooth days at work. No hot, erotic nights at home. He was alone everywhere he turned.

That was the way he liked it. That was the way he had crafted his life.

At least he had the baby.

Taking Jared's advice was virtually impossible. Dani tried, she really did. She checked off all the items on her vacation-days to-do list one by one. But eventually, her apartment was spotless. Her closets were an efficiency expert's dream, and she had made it through not one but two block-buster movies at the theater and couldn't have done a recap if she'd been under oath. The hours crawled by.

Friday morning, she caved. With trembling fingers, she picked up her cell phone and called the main line at New Century Tech. When the receptionist answered, Dani cleared her throat. "May I speak to Nathaniel Winston, please?"

The woman's voice was perky. "I'm so sorry, ma'am. Mr. Winston won't be in today. May I give you his voice mail?"

"No, thanks. It will keep till next week."

She hung up and gnawed the edge of her fingernail. Nathaniel Workaholic Winston had taken a day off? It didn't compute. Quickly, she ran through all the scenarios. Maybe he had the flu. Maybe the baby was sick. Maybe Ophelia had eluded investigators.

Or perhaps the baby had been returned to her mother, and Nathaniel was now headed for the Caribbean and a much-needed diving trip to unwind.

In the absence of hard facts, Dani didn't know what to do. In her mind, she had seen herself marching into New Century Tech armed with righteous indignation and confronting the wretched man on familiar ground. She definitely didn't want to go to the one place where she had first been intimate with him.

Memories of Christmas weekend made her shiver with a combination of yearning and dread. For those three days, she had lived in a dream world where Nathaniel needed and wanted her. But it had been a charade. A pleasant fiction.

Today was reality. The only choice left was to venture into enemy territory.

She had laundered the clothes Nathaniel bought for her and tucked them in a corner of her closet where she wouldn't have to think about him. Instead of couture items, today she chose from her own carefully curated wardrobe.

Appearance was important. She wanted to look confidant and poised. If there was any hope of convincing Nathaniel to give their relationship a fair hearing, she had to maintain control of her emotions *and* the confrontation.

He owed her an apology. Beyond that, she desperately hoped he owed her some kind of admission that he wanted more from her. More from them. Despite what he had told her about his childhood and adolescence, she refused to believe his heart was as impenetrable as he pretended.

She had watched him with Peaches. Seen the tenderness. The protectiveness. Nathaniel had a deep capacity for caring, even if he didn't recognize it. There was more to him than the hard-edged businessman who refused to be manipulated.

At least she hoped so. Hope was all she had left at this point.

In the end, she chose a work outfit. Black pencil skirt, royal blue sleeveless silk top and a matching waist-length jacket. The temps had remained balmy since the thaw, so she omitted tights and added her favorite pair of black flats. Her hair was cooperating for once. She brushed it vigorously and left it down.

The snow was completely gone by now, though the ground remained damp and mushy. Spring came early to Atlanta. It wouldn't be many weeks before daffodils began popping up. When she slid behind the wheel of her little car, it was impossible not to compare it to Nathaniel's Mercedes or the Hummer or even the helicopter.

None of those things were requirements for her happiness. As nice as it was to be pampered with fancy clothes and pricey transportation and a luxurious condo, they meant nothing in the end. It was the man she wanted, the man she needed. Even if he lost everything he had built from the ground up, just as his father had, the man at the helm of NCT would be more than enough for Dani.

She found a parking space on the street and fed the meter. Nathaniel's building was not someplace she could simply sashay into and catch a ride upstairs. Fortunately for her, Reggie was on duty.

He gave her a broad smile. "Hey there, Ms. Meadows. How was your holiday with the family?"

"Wonderful. And your clan?"

"Can't complain."

She gave him a conspiratorial smile. "I was hoping to surprise Mr. Winston. Do you mind letting me go up without telling him I'm on the way?"

His smile faded. "Mr. Winston's a tough customer, ma'am. He goes by the book. I can't afford to lose my job."

Squashing her panicky, guilty feelings, she nodded. "I understand. But you have my solemn word that if anything were to happen, I'd vouch for you. I'd tell him I slipped past you when you weren't looking." She stopped and decided to be honest. "We had an argument. A bad one. He's being bullheaded. Please. If he slams the door in my face, I'll leave and won't come back, I swear."

The man shifted from one foot to the other. "Let me call him first."

Damn it. She knew what the answer would be. "Never mind," she said dully. "I'll catch him at work next week." With the one tiny bit of hope she had amassed crushed into nothingness, she turned and headed for the street.

"Wait." Reggie called out to her, but not before her hand was on the glass door.

She turned around. "Yes?"

"I'll do it. I'll let you go up. I've seen how that man looks at you."

"You will? You have?"

The too-overweight-to-run security guard in his navy serge uniform and wrinkled white shirt nodded glumly. "Women. Y'all are pretty to look at, but sometimes you twist a man in knots. No offense, ma'am."

"None taken." She beamed at him. "Thank you. Thank you."

He grimaced. "Don't thank me yet. I've seen that gentleman angry. I hope you know what you're doing."

She didn't. Not at all. In the elevator, she trained her gaze on the neon-lit strip above the doors and watched the numbers increase. At last, the elevator swished to a smooth stop, a distant bell dinged and the doors opened.

Unfortunately, she'd left her stomach behind somewhere, several floors below.

Smoothing her damp palms on her skirt, she hitched the narrow strap of her modest purse higher on her shoulder and said a little prayer. Then she pressed the buzzer and waited.

Long moments later, the door swung open. Nathaniel stood there staring at her with narrowed eyes, naked from the waist up. He wore dress pants and socks and shoes, but his broad, tanned, really spectacular chest was bare.

"What do you want, Dani? I'm busy."

His expression could have frozen the sun.

She refused to take a step backward. "I need to talk to you. It's important."

"I'm not giving you your job back." Now his glare held a lick of heat.

"I'm not here about the job."

A sound from the other room drew his attention. "Fifteen minutes," he said. He strode away, leaving her to follow him in confusion.

In the den, she found Peaches, happily sitting in a wide-based contraption with music knobs and chew toys and other brightly colored amusements. The baby chortled as if she recognized Dani. Dani crouched and tickled the little girl's cheeks. "Hey, honey bunch. Did you miss me?"

Nathaniel stood in silence, frowning, his arms crossed over his chest.

She noticed several things at once—number one, a pale blue dress shirt tossed over the arm of the sofa. It was covered in infant cereal, presumably from the bowl of congealing goo on the coffee table. No fire burned in the grate. The small Christmas tree was gone.

Rising to her feet, she eyed him calmly. "I take it they haven't found Ophelia?"

"That's not really your concern, Dani. Say what you have to say and get out."

He wasn't making this easy. Hostility. Impatience. Barely disguised anger.

When her chin started to tremble, she locked her knees, clasped her hands at her waist and bit down hard on her bottom lip. The pain made her focus. "The reason I was sending out résumés is because I was attracted to you. I knew we couldn't work together under those conditions."

Not by even the flicker of an eyelash did he betray a response.

"Did you hear what I said?"

He shrugged. "It's a nice story."

"You owe me an apology," she said firmly.

Dark eyes glowed with heat. "The hell you say. I wasn't the one sneaking around."

"Don't use that snotty tone with me," she shot back. "You're hardly a saint."

"I'll give you that one. But at least I've been honest with you. Which is more than you can say in return."

She inhaled sharply, taking the biggest gamble of her life. "No," she said bluntly. "You haven't been honest with me at all."

His jaw dropped. "Of course I have."

"You have feelings for me. You might even love

me. But you're too scared to let me get close. The reason you freaked out when you heard I was looking for another job was that I hurt your feelings. And maybe you thought I was abandoning you. But I wasn't. I'm not."

"Don't flatter yourself, Dani. Women come and women go. You're no different from the rest."

"Nice speech. Have you been practicing?"

The lightning flash of fury in his gaze told her she might have gone too far.

Peaches played happily between them, her innocent baby noises a bizarre backdrop to the gravity of the moment.

Nathaniel ran a hand through his hair, a gesture indicating he was perhaps no calmer than she was. "Did you know NCT will be having a VP opening in the spring? McCaffrey is moving to the West Coast to care for his ailing parents. I had decided to recommend you for the spot. I'm sure with your new degree and your depth of experience at NCT, the board would have agreed."

"*Had* decided?" she asked faintly.

"Definitely past tense. You're the one who chose to leave." He picked up the baby who had begun to fuss. "It's time for her nap. Feel free to let yourself out."

When he returned several minutes later, Dani glared at him. "You're an ass, you know that?" Frustration clogged her throat.

"And you're an opportunist."

"Let me get this straight," she said tightly. "I produced a blizzard, planted a baby carrier on your car and arranged for myself to become indispensable to you so you would fall for my charms and I wouldn't have to leave?"

"I have no idea what goes through your mind. All I can say for sure is that you tried to manipulate me, but it won't happen. I won't let it, Dani. You can take your stories about *falling in love*— and peddle them elsewhere."

He was goading her. Trying to hurt her. And it was working. But the bitter ridicule was his defense mechanism. No one in his personal life had ever put him first. Through no fault of their own, his parents had abandoned him emotionally. Seeing his father's downfall after cheating with a coworker had cemented the idea that women— and lovers in particular—couldn't be trusted.

And then came Ophelia's manipulations. Poor Nathaniel. Beset at every turn.

Dani refused to back down or look away. In that intense moment, she saw the truth. He *was* feeling something. And it looked a lot like despair and yearning. Could it be true?

Clinging to the hope that what they had shared in this very room was more than lust and opportunity, she went to him and placed both hands, palms flat on his chest. The soft, springy hair beneath her fingertips was like silk. His flesh was hot and smooth.

He sucked in a startled breath when she touched him and then went rigid. "Get out," he said, the words hoarse, barely audible.

Dani shook her head. "I can't," she said softly. "Everything I need is right here. Maybe you don't believe me today. And maybe not tomorrow or the next day or the next. It doesn't matter. I'll keep telling you again and again as long as it takes."

She went up on her tiptoes, cradled his face in her hands and kissed him. "I love you, Nathaniel Winston. You're hard and stubborn and suspicious, but you're also intelligent and decent,

268 BILLIONAIRE BOSS, HOLIDAY BABY

and you have a deep capacity for love even if you don't know it. How many men would take in a baby who's probably not even his and care for her despite the havoc she wreaks in his life?"

She kissed him one more time. For a moment, she thought she had won. His hand cupped the back of her head, pulling her close and holding her as he responded to her kiss with bruising desperation.

But it didn't last. He jerked free and wiped his mouth with the back of his hand. "What would you say if I told you Peaches really is mine after all? That her real name is Lila, and that her mother doesn't want her...that Ophelia has signed away her rights because she's leaving the country with a man who doesn't tolerate children. What then, Dani? What if I said I'd marry you, but only with an ironclad prenup that puts everything in trust for the child?"

Stumbling backward in shock, she sank onto the sofa. She looked at the baby and back at Nathaniel. "It's true? She's yours?"

He didn't say a word. He simply stared at her with an expression she couldn't read.

Well, here was her choice. Nathaniel needed a

mother for his new daughter. Apparently, he was willing to spin the game to his advantage. Dani swallowed hard. "I'm very happy for you," she whispered. "I know you'll be a wonderful father."

Tears clogged her throat. She couldn't do it. She couldn't marry him knowing he didn't want her the same way she wanted him. It would destroy her.

Before coming here today, she had hoped to look into his eyes and see the truth about what he felt for her. She had told herself even a little flicker of love could grow.

If there was nothing in his feelings for Dani but lust, she was better off without him. She had to clear her throat twice before she could speak. "I'd take that deal in a heartbeat if you loved me. But you don't, do you?"

She stood on shaky legs and composed her expression. "I won't bother you again, Nathaniel. I wish you and Peaches all the best."

Rapidly, she walked out of the room, her heart beating in her chest so wildly she felt sick. Yanking open the door in the foyer that led to the hallway, she wiped her eyes, intending to flee, but Nathaniel was right on her heels.

"That's it?" he shouted. "You lose your shot at the money, and you're gone?"

"No," she said raggedly, turning to face him, tears spilling over and wetting her face. "I didn't lose. The truth is, I had a narrow escape. I don't want your money or your sterile condo or your stupidly expensive vehicles. I wanted a man who would love me. That's all. Now, forgive me for being slow, but I've finally figured out that man isn't you. You're going to live alone and die alone. I feel sorry for you, actually."

"I don't need your pity," he snarled.

She reached blindly for the doorknob, desperate to escape. A hard masculine hand came down on her shoulder, spinning her around. Nathaniel's face was white, his eyes glittering like coals.

"Let me go," she cried.

He got up in her face, his breath warm on her cheeks, his grip on her shoulders viselike. "What makes you think you can save me from myself?"

And then she saw it. Buried beneath the layers of fury and condemnation was a pained uncertainty. Nathaniel Winston thought he was unlovable.

Her whole body went limp. She could fight his

pigheadedness but not such aching vulnerability from a man who prided himself on icy control. She could barely breathe.

"I was hoping we could save each other," she whispered. The time for self-preservation was gone. She would give him complete honesty or nothing at all. "The world is a scary place, Nathaniel. But when I'm with you, everything seems possible. I didn't want to fall in love. That's why I was leaving NCT. But I waited too long and the snow came, and now I can't imagine waking up every morning and not seeing your face."

Thirteen

Nathaniel still reeled from the shock of finding out he was a father, and now Dani expected him to believe the two of them had a chance?

He shoved her away and paced the confines of the foyer, feeling sick. "Love makes a man stupid," he muttered. "Did you see all that baby stuff I bought? I'm a sucker."

Dani stood watching him with pity in her eyes, her arms wrapped around her waist. He didn't need that, not from her. She looked beautiful and professional and exactly like the woman who had worked with him for almost two years. But things had changed.

She lifted her shoulders and let them fall. "You'll be a better parent than either your father *or* your mother was if you put your mind to it. I'm sorry Ophelia abandoned her daughter."

Rage filled his chest. "People shouldn't have babies if they can't follow through. It's criminal."

His ragged shout echoed in the small foyer. Dani stared at him, her blue eyes awash in tears. "I can't make up for what you lost, Nathaniel. I wish to God it was possible. But we could do it right this time. Peaches doesn't have to be the only one. Families are wonderful."

He blinked, not sure what he was hearing. After every cruel, heartless thing he had said to her? He cleared his throat, his head spinning. "Are you offering to give me a baby?"

Her chin wobbled. "No. I'm saying I want to *make* a baby with you. When the time is right." She tried to smile, but the failed attempt broke his heart. "I love you. Even though you're acting like a jackass and trying to shove me out the door, I won't stop loving you. I'll sign a legal document if you need a tangible reason to trust me."

Fear like he had never known clutched him from every angle. Spending time with Dani's parents and siblings had shown him what normal family life could look like. The yearning had hit him hard, reminding of everything his mother's illness had cost him.

"I lied to you, Dani," he muttered, stung by the enormity of his sins.

She frowned. "About what?"

"You asked me if I had ever fantasized about you at the office."

She paled. "You told me you *had*."

"That was an understatement," he said flatly. "The truth was too damning."

"I don't understand."

"Six months after you first started working with me, I began dreaming about you. Every night. In vivid Technicolor."

Her eyes widened. "Oh."

He shrugged. "It scared the hell out of me. I'd watched my father go down that road and be ripped apart financially and emotionally. For years, I told myself I would never get involved with an employee. But there you were, so bright and funny and damned good at the job. I was stuck. Every day you and I worked together like the proverbial well-oiled machine, and every night I undressed you a thousand times and a thousand ways in my mind."

"So it wasn't just me…" Her eyes were round.

He shuddered, wanting her desperately and yet afraid to touch her. "No."

"Are you in love with me, Nathaniel?"

The words were barely audible. Maybe she was scared, but she didn't show it. The stupid woman didn't know how to protect herself. "Men like fucking," he said. "We don't wrap it up in pretty ribbons."

He was testing her. Pushing her. Trying to drive her away.

Dani inhaled sharply and fell back a step as if his deliberate profanity were a physical blow. "So you would rather have a temporary affair?"

"Are you available?" He stared at his nemesis, stone-faced. Every emotion he felt for her hammered in his chest like a wild swarm of butterflies trying desperately to break free.

In the hushed silence, he witnessed the moment Dani saw past his facade. Her expression softened.

"For one night," she said softly, her face aglow as if she heard something amazing in his crude offer. She was young but wise. Sure of herself and maybe of him, as well. "And the next and the next and all the ones after that."

"Fine," he said. His hands trembled, so he jammed them in his pockets. "Don't most women want a man down on one knee? The pricey ring. The pretty speeches? I'm surprised you're selling yourself short."

"Shut up, Nathaniel." Her wry smile warmed him from the inside out. "Shut up and prove to me I'm not making the biggest mistake of my life." She wrapped her arms around his waist and laid her cheek exactly over the spot where his heart pounded madly.

His hands tangled in her hair. He couldn't stop shaking. It was a mostly unmanly thing to do, but Dani didn't seem to mind. He clutched her tightly. "I don't know how to do forever."

She went up on her tiptoes and pressed her lips to his. "We'll figure it out together," she said. "It won't be so bad, Nathaniel, I promise."

The walls came down, every brick, every fragment of mortar. He inhaled her scent, his mind a blank. "I need you, my sweet Christmas elf."

"I know," Dani whispered. "I know…"

Epilogue

Thirty-six hours later, New Year's Eve

Nathaniel flung open the door to his condo and dropped a pile of packages on the chair in the foyer. "I'm home," he yelled.

Dani appeared, her radiant smile catching him unawares and wiping every coherent thought from his brain. "What took you so long?" she said.

He scooped her up and twirled her in dizzying circles until her hair fanned out from her head and they both laughed breathlessly. "It's not easy finding a Christmas tree on December 31." He released her and grabbed up the largest bag. "What do you think?"

The tree was prelit, but that was its only claim to fame. Twelve inches high and already shedding artificial needles, it was a tree only a mother could love...or a man bent on setting the stage for romance.

"I adore it," Dani said, her eyes dancing with amusement.

"Help me carry everything." he said. He headed straight for the den and began setting out his bounty. Carryout containers from Dani's favorite restaurant. An eighty-dollar bottle of champagne. Tulips and roses from a ridiculously expensive Buckhead florist.

Dani plugged in the tiny tree and set it on the hearth, then stood back and watched, her expression caught somewhere between excitement and apprehension. The two of them had spent the majority of yesterday afternoon and evening making love. Nathaniel had slept the entire night with her in his arms. This morning they had made French toast together.

Now came the hard part.

When he was finished with the accoutrements,

he examined his handiwork. He'd never tried to impress a woman before, not really. Tonight, it was vital that Dani understand what was happening.

He took her hand. "We need to talk." Fortunately, Peaches was asleep at the moment.

Dani blinked. "Ouch. Barely a day and a half and we already need to *talk*?"

Drawing her over to the sofa, he sat down and pointed to the opposite end. "You, there," he said. He had important things to say. His self-control was tenuous at best, so he wasn't taking any chances.

She cooperated obediently, leaning back into the corner embrace of his expensive leather sofa and crisscrossing her legs like a child. Her hair was clean and damp and shiny. He knew she had showered while he was gone, because he smelled the soap his housekeeper put in the bathrooms.

They had stopped by Dani's apartment late yesterday, so now she had her own wardrobe to choose from. Tonight she was wearing gray leggings and an off-the-shoulder, cotton-candy-pink sweater. Her feet were bare. There was a good chance she wasn't wearing a bra. He didn't look too closely, because if she weren't, he might forget his speech.

Dani held out her hands, palms up. "The food is getting cold, Nathaniel. Say whatever you have to say."

Her lips smiled, but her gaze was wary. That expression in her eyes crucified him. How long would it take before she ceased expecting the worst from him?

He jumped to his feet and paced. For the past hour, he'd rehearsed what he wanted to say. Now, suddenly, his brain fogged. "You were right to say I owed you an apology. Looking for other employment was a very professional thing for you to do. But the prospect of you not being in the office every day caught me off guard. I never wanted you to resign, not really. I was angry, and I lashed out." His stomach cramped. "You have an incredible brain and the ability to connect with all kinds of people. I would hate to see you leave NCT. You deserve the chance to prove what you can do for the company."

"I see."

"You already said that once," he muttered.

"True." Dani gnawed her bottom lip. "Is what

I do at NCT more important to you than talking about us?"

"I didn't say that."

"I'm confused. Now that we're practicing dé-tente, I assumed our personal life was going to take precedence over work."

"It does. It will." He stopped and cleared his throat. "Maybe this will help." He reached inside the pocket of his jacket and pulled out a folded sheaf of papers. "Happy New Year, Dani. I may be the world's most stubborn man, but I believe in second chances, and I hope you do, too. That's not a prenup, by the way," he said hastily.

She unfolded the papers and stared at them, turning one page at a time slowly. Nathaniel had paid his expensive legal team a fat bonus to put the wheels in motion on his grand gesture before the clock struck midnight.

Dani throat worked. She refolded the document he had worked so hard to procure and handed it back to him. "No. No, Nathaniel. I won't take it."

He had signed over half his company to her. A partnership holding in NCT. It was a small enough price to pay for her willingness to for-give him and promise him a future.

His face heated. "I don't know what you want from me, damn it. How many ways do I have to say it?"

Dani jumped to her feet and scowled. "You haven't even said it once, you big blockhead. I never wanted your life's work. All I want is to hear you tell me the truth."

Ah, hell. The shakes came back. "You know how I feel about you," he said gruffly.

She shook her head slowly. "Not good enough, Winston. Try again."

"Marry me," he blurted.

"Why?"

His throat closed up. Sweat broke out on his forehead. "I can't explain. It won't make sense."

"Try me," she said gently.

He fell to his knees on the thick, plush carpet and wrapped his arms around her hips, resting his cheek against her belly. "I want to feel him here," he said. "Our son, or maybe another daughter, kicking and making herself known. I want her to know she is loved from the moment she takes her first breath."

Dani's hands tangled in his hair. "Is that all?"

He shook his head, his throat tight. "No. I want her to know how much I love her mother."

Dani knelt as well and kissed him softly. "That wasn't so difficult, was it? You're going to have to practice," she whispered, tears streaming down her face. "I'm not going to drag it out of you every time I need to hear it."

He rested his forehead against hers. "I adore you. I want you. I'll love you for a hundred years. I was afraid of this. Afraid of you…"

"And now?"

"Now you're my heart, my home," he said simply. "Everything I ever wanted and more. I'm never letting go…"

* * * * *

MILLS & BOON®
Large Print – November 2017

ROMANCE

The Pregnant Kavakos Bride — Sharon Kendrick
The Billionaire's Secret Princess — Caitlin Crews
Sicilian's Baby of Shame — Carol Marinelli
The Secret Kept from the Greek — Susan Stephens
A Ring to Secure His Crown — Kim Lawrence
Wedding Night with Her Enemy — Melanie Milburne
Salazar's One-Night Heir — Jennifer Hayward
The Mysterious Italian Houseguest — Scarlet Wilson
Bound to Her Greek Billionaire — Rebecca Winters
Their Baby Surprise — Katrina Cudmore
The Marriage of Inconvenience — Nina Singh

HISTORICAL

Ruined by the Reckless Viscount — Sophia James
Cinderella and the Duke — Janice Preston
A Warriner to Rescue Her — Virginia Heath
Forbidden Night with the Warrior — Michelle Willingham
The Foundling Bride — Helen Dickson

MEDICAL

Mummy, Nurse...Duchess? — Kate Hardy
Falling for the Foster Mum — Karin Baine
The Doctor and the Princess — Scarlet Wilson
Miracle for the Neurosurgeon — Lynne Marshall
English Rose for the Sicilian Doc — Annie Claydon
Engaged to the Doctor Sheikh — Meredith Webber

MILLS & BOON®
Hardback – December 2017

ROMANCE

His Queen by Desert Decree	Lynne Graham
A Christmas Bride for the King	Abby Green
Captive for the Sheikh's Pleasure	Carol Marinelli
Legacy of His Revenge	Cathy Williams
A Night of Royal Consequences	Susan Stephens
Carrying His Scandalous Heir	Julia James
Christmas at the Tycoon's Command	Jennifer Hayward
Innocent in the Billionaire's Bed	Clare Connelly
Snowed in with the Reluctant Tycoon	Nina Singh
The Magnate's Holiday Proposal	Rebecca Winters
The Billionaire's Christmas Baby	Marion Lennox
Christmas Bride for the Boss	Kate Hardy
Christmas with the Best Man	Susan Carlisle
Navy Doc on Her Christmas List	Amy Ruttan
Christmas Bride for the Sheikh	Carol Marinelli
Her Knight Under the Mistletoe	Annie O'Neil
The Nurse's Special Delivery	Louisa George
Her New Year Baby Surprise	Sue MacKay
His Secret Son	Brenda Jackson
Best Man Under the Mistletoe	Jules Bennett

MILLS & BOON®
Large Print – November 2017

ROMANCE

An Heir Made in the Marriage Bed	Anne Mather
The Prince's Stolen Virgin	Maisey Yates
Protecting His Defiant Innocent	Michelle Smart
Pregnant at Acosta's Demand	Maya Blake
The Secret He Must Claim	Chantelle Shaw
Carrying the Spaniard's Child	Jennie Lucas
A Ring for the Greek's Baby	Melanie Milburne
The Runaway Bride and the Billionaire	Kate Hardy
The Boss's Fake Fiancée	Susan Meier
The Millionaire's Redemption	Therese Beharrie
Captivated by the Enigmatic Tycoon	Bella Bucannon

HISTORICAL

Marrying His Cinderella Countess	Louise Allen
A Ring for the Pregnant Debutante	Laura Martin
The Governess Heiress	Elizabeth Beacon
The Warrior's Damsel in Distress	Meriel Fuller
The Knight's Scarred Maiden	Nicole Locke

MEDICAL

Healing the Sheikh's Heart	Annie O'Neil
A Life-Saving Reunion	Alison Roberts
The Surgeon's Cinderella	Susan Carlisle
Saved by Doctor Dreamy	Dianne Drake
Pregnant with the Boss's Baby	Sue MacKay
Reunited with His Runaway Doc	Lucy Clark

MILLS & BOON®

Why shop at millsandboon.co.uk?

Each year, thousands of romance readers find their perfect read at millsandboon.co.uk. That's because we're passionate about bringing you the very best romantic fiction. Here are some of the advantages of shopping at www.millsandboon.co.uk:

* **Get new books first**—you'll be able to buy your favourite books one month before they hit the shops

* **Get exclusive discounts**—you'll also be able to buy our specially created monthly collections, with up to 50% off the RRP

* **Find your favourite authors**—latest news, interviews and new releases for all your favourite authors and series on our website, plus ideas for what to try next

* **Join in**—once you've bought your favourite books, don't forget to register with us to rate, review and join in the discussions

Visit **www.millsandboon.co.uk**
for all this and more today!